"Sonar contact," Borodine yelled, "bearing one-oh-eight relative. Range eighteen thousand yards. It's an attack sub, *Alfa* class. Codename *Abbott*. And, she's silent."

"Battle stations!" Admiral Jack Boxer ordered. "Bastards are lying in the weeds for us. Come to—"

"Small transients on screen, Skipper. Four torpedo spread. Closing at two thousand yards. Ninety seconds to impact."

"All ahead flank. Blow remaining positive. Crash dive at one thousand. Arm Sea Darts and plot firing solution."

A chorus of responses rang out. In less than a minute, the *Seawolf* was roaring downward at an unbelievably steep angle.

"Standing by with Darts, sir."

"On my command . . . launch Darts!"

"Sea Darts away. Estimated impact, forty-five seconds!"

There was a sudden screaming silence in the control room as the projectiles zeroed in. Boxer and his crew sweated the seconds to impact. Then, the indicators went wild.

"Hit. We have a hit on Sea Dart One, sir."

"Confirm hit?"

There was a pause and all eyes in the CR went to the sonar station. After a minute, Borodine pulled off his headset and turned to Boxer. "Hit confirmed. Sea Dart Two detonation close aboard the first. *Abbott* is dead!"

DEPTH FORCE

#16: RIG WAR

IRVING A. GREENFIELD

ZEBRA BOOKS
KENSINGTON PUBLISHING CORP.

ZEBRA BOOKS

are published by

Kensington Publishing Corp.
475 Park Avenue South
New York, NY 10016

First printing: August, 1992

Printed in the United States of America

Chapter One

Boxer looked at the sonar display; there were a half dozen surface ships around the SSN-S1, including one carrier, the recently refurbished *America*.

"I'm surprised there isn't an attack sub out there," Commander Sarkis said, coming alongside Boxer to look at the display.

Boxer laughed. "If we try to make a run for it, you can bet there'll be more than one. . . . Make no mistake, they're 'out there,' just beyond the range of our sonar."

"Probably," Sarkis answered.

Boxer stepped away from the master control console, and calmly said, "We'll surface."

Sarkis hesitated.

"We've accomplished our mission," Boxer said. "I'm not looking for a shootout that we can't possibly win."

"If we made a run for the Arctic . . ."

Boxer shook his head. "It has to be this way. We don't really have a choice." After a momentary pause, he said, "On the standard open channel have COMMO send this message . . . To the governments of the world, the hot zone in the North Pacific Ocean has been destroyed, Admiral Jack Boxer and the Crew of the SSN-S1."

"Yes, sir," Sarkis answered.

"And immediately after that send this. . . . To the Commander of the United States surface squadron — give our precise latitude and longitude to the nearest tenth of a second — this is Admiral Jack Boxer. The SSN-S1 will surface in ten minutes, 0923, local time, and surrender. Other than the crew be treated as prisoners of war under the Geneva Convention, no terms are asked."

"You want that sent —"

"On the open channel . . . just in case someone topside is trigger-happy," Boxer said.

Sarkis nodded.

Boxer gave a slight smile, then walked back to the MCC, switched on the 1MC, and said, "Now hear this . . . all hands, now hear this. . . . This is Admiral Boxer speaking . . . In exactly ten minutes from now, we will surface and surrender ourselves to the commander of the American squadron. . . . It has been an honor to serve on the same vessel with you, and it has been a greater honor to count all of you as my shipmates." To allow himself time to clear his voice and take a deep breath, he momentarily switched off the 1MC. Then, when it was on again, he said, "All hands, now hear this . . . all hands, now hear this. . . . Standby to surface . . . standby to surface."

Boxer switched off the 1MC and, pressing the red Klaxon control button, held it for several seconds.

Admiral Peter Kirkson read the message twice, and

looked up at Commander Host, a tall, broad-shouldered, twenty year man. Kirkson roared, "Just what the fuck does this mean?"

Before Host could answer, a junior officer on the admiral's staff said, "Excuse me, sir, you have another message from CINCPAC."

Host took the message, nodded, and returned the salute of the junior officer.

"Read the damn thing out loud," Kirkson growled.

Host scanned the message, looked at Kirkson and said, "Sir, I think you had better read this yourself."

Kirkson took the blue lightweight paper, and read it. "Christ, the President has ordered that Boxer and his crew be treated as if they were prisoners of war."

"Yes, sir," Host answered.

Kirkson began to pace the width of the flag bridge. He was a tall, lean man with high cheekbones, flashing brown eyes, and graying brown hair. For him a man like Boxer was a disgrace to the Navy. He went by the book; any officer who didn't, was, in his opinion, either pandering to gain the popularity of the men, or a glory seeker. Maybe both. He believed that Boxer was guilty of doing both things.

"Alright, if that's the way the game is going to be played, then we'll play it by the book."

Host answered, "Yes, sir."

"I want two choppers out, ready to take up positions off the boat's starboard and port sides as soon as she surfaces. I want them in close and low," Kirkson said.

"Sir—"

"Yes, I know that it will send water all over the deck, but my guess is that Boxer will have his men stand at attention. I don't want the damn TV people to see them as sailors. I want them to look like drowned rats."

"I understand, sir."

"Have two squads of marines board the boat. The prisoners will immediately be transferred by launch to this ship, where they will strip down on deck, and be issued work clothes."

"Officers?"

"They will be separated from the crew, taken to a different part of the flight deck, but treated exactly the same way," Kirkson said.

"Sir, with a wind chill factor—"

"You have my orders," Kirkson said gruffly.

"Yes, sir."

"Under no circumstance is any member of the crew to speak, or communicate with the prisoners."

"The members of the press—"

"All access to either the men or the officers of the SSN-S1 is denied," Kirkson said. "I don't want them made into heroes on the six o'clock news."

Host said nothing.

"I will not tolerate any coddling of these . . . these pirates," Kirkson told his aide.

"No, sir," Host agreed. Then, with his face totally expressionless, he asked, "Sir, do you want them in chains?"

"What?"

Host repeated the question keeping his face expressionless.

After a moment, during which he stared intently at his aide in an effort to divine the true nature of the question and failing, Kirkson said, "I hope that wasn't intended as a joke, Commander?"

"No, sir," Host answered.

"Then, would you please explain it?"

"Sir, according to regulation twenty nine, paragraph—"

"Yes, yes, get to the point, Commander."

"Under the regulations you have the right to keep them in chains," Host answered.

Kirkson began to pace again, then stopped abruptly, facing Host. "If I knew that Washington wouldn't come down on me like a ton of bricks, you bet that I'd chain those bastards."

"Yes, sir."

A junior officer approached the two of them, saluted and said, "Sirs, the SSN-S1 will surface in approximately three minutes."

"On which side?"

"Port, sir. Approximately five hundred yards away from us. Sonar reports she's just holding steerageway."

"Get those choppers out," Kirkson said, looking straight at Host.

"Yes, sir," Host answered, saluted, and immediately went to the bank of phones on the flag bridge.

Kirkson moved to the starboard side of the bridge. Far below him, the dark waters of the North Pacific heaved under a leaden sky. Despite the fact that he had not seen the 0600 weather advisory, his years of experience as a fighter pilot and ship captain gave him an insight into the subtle changes of sea and sky that predicted the coming of a storm. He could, as the old saw goes, smell it. He pushed the gray sky and dark waters out of his conscious thoughts, and concentrated on the drama that was beginning to unfold.

"Sir," Host said, coming up behind Kirkson, "choppers will launch in one minute."

"Get a weather update," Kirkson said, without turning.

"Yes, sir."

Suddenly the ship's 1MC came on. "All hands, stand by . . . deck crew, prepare to launch chopper one . . . launch chopper one. All hands standby . . . deck crew, prepare to launch chopper two . . . launch chopper two."

Kirkson sat down in the captain's chair, and switched on the radio. "Chopper one, chopper two, this is Admiral Kirkson speaking. Acknowledge."

Both pilots answered that they heard him loud and clear.

Kirkson repeated the instruction that Host had given them. "I want you to stay close to the deck, and give the boat a good dousing."

"For how long, sir," the pilot of chopper one asked.

"Until the Marine detachment is aboard and the boat's crew is on its way to the *America*," Kirkson said, using the name of his flag ship.

"Wilco," both chopper pilots responded.

Kirkson took time to cut a cigar and lit it. He had never expected Boxer to attempt to fight his way out. He was disappointed that Boxer had not fought, and even more disappointed that the hero of so many battles had resorted to using his influence in Washington to protect himself and his crew. But he had certainly fantasized how he would have fought him. He'd have done it from the flag bridge. He'd have hunted him down, and then, when his attack submarine had found him, he would have sent in his planes armed with smaller and lighter versions of the Sea Darts to finish him off. . . .

"Sir, sonar reports target, bearing one eight zero.

Range five hundred yards. Depth fifty feet."

Kirkson switched on his sonar display, and at the same time contacted the two chopper pilots. "Standby to hover," he ordered.

Boxer watched the digital depth readout pass fifty feet. "Standby, all hands. Do not open hatches . . . repeat, do not open hatches."

In less than a minute, the SSN-S1 broke the surface of the icy North Pacific, and began to roll in response to the wind driven waves.

"Two choppers on either side of us, at fifty feet," the radar officer reported.

Boxer picked up a phone, and called the communications officer. "Give me a direct link with Admiral Kirkson," he said.

"Yes, sir," the COMMO answered.

Several moments passed before the COMMO reported, "Sir, the admiral has refused to speak with you."

Boxer ran his right hand over his chin, which was heavy with pepper and salt stubble, the beginning of the beard he intended to grow. He did not know Kirkson personally, but he did know *about* him. The Navy, despite its size, was a small society within the nation's larger one. Kirkson's reputation, though not as bad as some others, left much to be desired, more because of his rigidity than anything else. The standing joke about him was that when it came time to making love to his wife, he went by the numbers. Maybe that was why she'd left him for the psychiatrist she'd been seeing. . . .

"Tell, whoever is on the other end, that unless those choppers are returned to the carrier within five min-

11

utes, the SSN-S1 will dive again, and stay below until they are."

"Sir—"

"Send the same message to the CINCPAC and to the CNO," Boxer said.

There was a momentary pause on the other end.

"Send it!" Boxer ordered.

"Yes, sir."

Boxer returned the phone to its cradle, leaned back, and waited. If Kirkson wanted to play hard ball, he'd play it, but he'd play it Boxer's way. . . .

Kirkson read the flimsy handed to him by Host, who had gotten it from a lieutenant, who, in turn, had been in the flag's communication center when it had come in, and had been given the unhappy task of delivering it.

"Did you read this?" Kirkson said, his face going to a deep red.

"Scanned it, sir," Host replied.

"By Jesus, I'll blow the son of a bitch out of the water," Kirkson stormed.

Host remained silent.

"Just what the fuck does he think we—"

"Sir, Admiral Boxer is one of those men who is always thinking," Host said.

Kirkson raised his eyebrows. "Are you suggesting that I accede to his demands?"

"Sir, I suggest nothing. The final decision is yours," Host said. "But—"

"But, what?"

"There are several dozen media people aboard, who are only waiting for some reason to make more of a hero out of Boxer and his men than they already have made of them."

Kirkson began to pace the flag bridge, while Host motioned the lieutenant away.

Suddenly, Kirkson halted, turned, and faced Host. "Order the chopper back to the ship," he said.

"Yes, sir," Host answered.

Boxer watched the two blips on the radar screen rise, bank to the right, and head back to the ship. He smiled, and switching the 1MC, he said, "All hands, now hear this . . . change to dress uniform immediately . . ." he paused, before he added, "We want to give the media the kind of show they expect." Then, switching off the 1MC, he turned to Sarkis. "The tough part will come later. Now, it's fun."

"Some *fun*," Sarkis answered gloomily.

"Well, look at it this way. When was the last time you were arrested for piracy?"

Sarkis shook his head, but didn't say anything.

Slapping him on the back, Boxer said, "Listen, you did the world a good turn. Few men have the opportunity to do that. Now, the worse thing that can happen to you is that you will be imprisoned for the rest of your life, or that you will be executed. Anything else will be gravy."

"Thanks for making my future look so rosy," Sarkis responded.

"Anytime," Boxer said, and then suggested that they change into their dress uniforms.

"I think you're really enjoying this."

"Maybe, or maybe I'm trying to make the best of a

situation that puts all of us into not 'the best of all possible worlds.' Besides, if the weather worsens any more, we'll dive and wait it out."

Kirkson studied the deck of the SSN-S1. None of the hatches had been opened, and the boat was just holding steerageway. He turned to Host, "Now, what the hell is going on?"

"Sir, I don't know. But if nothing happens soon we're going to be in some bad weather. There's a storm coming in, and it's a big one."

"Storm?" Kirkson questioned.

"Yes, sir. We've been tracking it since yesterday."

Kirkson remembered having become bodily aware of it, but he'd been so preoccupied with Boxer's imminent surrender that he'd pushed the scent of the storm into the limbo regions of his mind. Quickly, he focused on it. "Where is it now? What's its speed and course?"

Host said, "Last report places its leading edge twelve miles from our position, speed thirty miles an hour, and increasing."

Kirkson looked at the sea, during the last few minutes it had become heavier. "I want Boxer and damn crew aboard, now," he fumed.

"Yes, sir," Host responded, and immediately went to the phone that connected him directly to Marine Captain Frank Geron, who commanded the ship's Marine detachment, and gave him his orders. Then, he added, in a much lower tone, "Good luck."

"We'll need it in this weather," the Marine captain answered.

Host put the phone down, and returned to where

14

Kirkson was. "They'll be away in five minutes, sir," he said.

"He's playing a game," Kirkson growled, now very much aware of the storm.

"Who, sir?" Host asked, pretending not to know who the admiral meant. But before Kirkson could answer, two men appeared on the boat's bridge, and a moment later its 1MC system came on.

"This is Admiral Boxer. Do not launch your Marine detachment. Call it back. The sea is too rough. You will not be able to take us in tow, or put another crew aboard."

Kirkson's face crimsoned. "What?" he roared. He switched on the 1MC. "This is Admiral Kirkson, you are to surrender immediately."

"To prevent a possible accident, or loss of life, we will submerge until the storm abates, then we will surface, and the marines can come aboard."

"Negative," Kirkson shouted. But the SSN-S1 was already beginning to dive. "I don't fucking believe this is happening."

Host remained silent, but he very much wanted to laugh.

"Make one hundred," Boxer ordered, reentering the CR. "Sarkis, radio our friend topside and our other friends who work CINCPAC and Washington, that we will remain at depth of one hundred feet, and maintain steerageway. "Tell—"

"Sir, the marines are in trouble," one of the other men said.

Boxer glanced at the TV screen. "Christ!" he exclaimed, and immediately shouted, "Blow negative!" He hit the Klaxon button three times. Then, over 1MC, he said, "Standby to surface . . . bridge detail, top side . . . emergency deck detail, port side."

The SSN-S1 regained the surface. The bridge hatch was thrown open, and the bridge detail took their stations.

Boxer was on the port side with the emergency deck detail. Using a bullhorn, he said, "Stand by to receive a line."

One of the men tossed a line to the marines in the launch, which was now almost below the surface of the raging sea.

"The line fell short," one of the submariners reported.

"Get that line to them," Boxer shouted over the howling wind.

The line went out again, and again fell short.

"Here, take this," Boxer said, giving one of the men the bullhorn. Then, taking the line, he wrapped it around his waist, made a bowline knot, and went over the side into the surging sea.

The launch was maybe sixty feet away from the boat. But the waves, some ten feet high or more, made the distance seem much greater to Boxer, even though he was a powerful swimmer.

Blinded by the surging water, Boxer momentarily treaded water, and cleared his eyes. Then, he struck out for the boat, which was still several yards away, and almost down in the water to its gunnels.

Suddenly, Boxer was there, alongside the foundering boat. "The line is around my waist. Get your men into the water, and get them on the line."

Geron shouted, "Over the side! Get hold of the line

. . . go, now!"

Moments later, the marines were hanging on to the line.

Boxer climbed into the boat, broke out the flare gun, loaded it and fired it, then he went over the side.

An instant later, the emergency deck detail began to pull the line back on to the SSN-S1.

Despite the slashing rain and the heavy seas, the eyes of the men on the flag bridge of the *America* were riveted on the drama that was being played out a scant five hundred feet from them.

"Pull, you bastards," shouted a yeoman.

Host clamped his jaws shut, lest he erupt with similar words.

"The first man is aboard!" a junior officer shouted.

Everyone, with the exception of Kirkson, broke into wild cheering.

"By God, that took real courage," Host finally said. "Real courage."

Before Kirkson could answer, the door to the bridge opened, and the Marine guard announced, "Mister Thomas Crieder requests permission to come on the bridge."

Host glanced at Kirkson, who shook his head.

"Permission—" Crieder was on the bridge before Kirkson could add the word denied.

"Admiral, that was the most spectacular thing I have seen in years. That man saved the lives of every man in that launch, and I have every bit of it on video tape. You wouldn't know his name, would you?"

"That was Admiral Jack Boxer," Host answered.

"Boxer?"

"Mister Crieder, you were not granted permission to enter the flag bridge," Kirkson said stiffly. "Please leave."

Crieder, a respected TV news anchorman, was not to be cowered by the likes of Kirkson. "Well, that's not gratitude or anything, is it?" he responded, smiling broadly.

"And what the hell is that supposed to mean, sir?" Kirkson asked.

"Well, sir, I was just about to invite you and your staff to a dinner I'm giving," Crieder answered.

"Dinner?"

"Yes, sir, the ship's skipper was kind enough to let me use his dining room for the occasion."

"And what, may I ask, is the occasion?"

Crieder smiled as if Kirkson were retarded, and he was patiently explaining a simple idea. "Naturally, to celebrate the courage of the Navy, as exemplified by the selfless courage of Admiral Jack Boxer and his men."

"Off this bridge," Kirkson roared, pointing to the door. "Off this bridge!"

Crieder nodded, and said, "Sir, our entire conversation has been taped." Then, he turned, and left the bridge.

"Sir, the SSN-S1 is submerging," a junior officer reported.

Kirkson ran to the forward window, and saw the very top of the SSN-S1's sail just slip below the gray, raging waters of the North Pacific Ocean.

Chapter Two

Eric Von Stempler was looking at a picture postcard view of the Swiss Alps from the window of his office on the twenty-seventh floor of the headquarters building for the World Wide Disposal Corporation on Bahnhoffstrasse in Zurich.

On the wall behind him, at the other side of the room, a battery of a dozen TV monitors displayed the machinations of the major stock, bond and commodity markets in as many major cities of the world. A huge computer installation located next to the TV tied him electronically to its many overseas operations.

Eric Von, as he enjoyed being called, was forty-eight years old, not quite six feet tall, and broad boned. His blue eyes belied a look of boyish innocence that was accentuated by his close-cropped blond hair. Distantly related to an infamous Nazi general, he cultivated a pseudo military bearing in his personal mannerisms that were carried over into his business dealings.

For the last hour, he had been monitoring the events that were occurring thousands of miles away in the North Pacific Ocean.

"And how long is that storm supposed to last?" Eric Von asked.

The disembodied voice of Arkady Tosenko came from a video phone speaker on the highly polished black teak wood desk directly behind him. Tosenko answered, "Twenty-four to seventy-two hours at the most."

Eric Von made a slow turn, looked at the video picture of the man on the other end, and scowled. "Where are your Russian submarines?" he asked.

"They are close by."

" 'Close by,' " Eric said, mimicking the man's Eastern European accent. "But not close enough to stop Boxer from destroying our—" he stopped. "Alright, what he did can't be undone. Our problem, now, is to make sure that he doesn't have the opportunity to do it again."

"Absolutely," Tosenko answered.

"Are you sure that the Americans will imprison him?"

"He's guilty of piracy, and that's a crime that calls for the death penalty."

Eric Von smiled. "That would certainly eliminate him," he said.

"The best he could hope for is life imprisonment."

"If money will buy either the death penalty or imprisonment for life, you have as much as you need."

"I understand," Tosenko said.

Eric Von faced the screen again. "We can't afford to have another disaster like the hot zone."

"I assure you there won't be one," Tosenko responded.

Eric Von remained silent. As far as he was concerned, the conversation was over. A few moments later Tosenko realized it, too, and the video phone screen went blank.

"The Java strike is the biggest oil field in the world, Mister President."

The President, a man of middling height, whose financial roots went deep into Texas oil, knew the economic importance of the Java strike. However, he was in the midst of a presidential election year, and had to contend with the problems Boxer caused to the party's environmental image. He left his chair and walked around to the front of the desk, which he was fond of sitting on. He addressed his chief of staff, Admiral Chris Fletcher, and Senate Minority Whip, Donald Johnston. "We need that damn oil. Boys, cut the deal that will get us that oil. But right now my problem is way over in the other end of the Pacific, and he's comin' home here to stand trial for a crime that everyone of us would have committed if faced with the same circumstance." He launched himself off the desk, and returned to his chair. "Not twenty minutes ago, he saved a whole boat load of marines, who were on their way to board the SSN-S1, and take him prisoner. It played to a worldwide TV audience; that man can't stop being a hero even when he has all the reason not to be one."

Fletcher and Johnston agreed, and Johnston went further by saying, "Luckily, he's not running for public office."

The President frowned at the not too subtle reminder that his popularity had waned since the end of summer. His approval rating plummeted when the nation's economy took a nosedive, and the Arab countries, who had the major share of the world's oil, took advantage of the situation by raising their price for crude. It was now at an all-time high of fifty-three dollars a barrel.

"Mister President, it is our opinion that the dissolution of the USSR and the consequent formation of a loose commonwealth of independent states has posed a very different kind of military threat," Admiral Fletcher said.

The President looked at him. "Make sure that it doesn't happen," he said sharply. "I want our satellite surveillance substantially increased. What I don't need *now* is trouble from that quarter."

Senator Johnston said, "Getting back to Boxer. I suggest that we allow the court-martial to go its way."

"Why?"

"Because there are many people whose concept of right and wrong make them less willing to acknowledge him as a hero, and see him more as a villain."

"What's your opinion, Fletch?" the President asked, moving his eyes from Johnston to the admiral.

Fletcher thought for a few moments before he answered, "I'd go with the flow. You know how fickle people can be. Once they find out more about his personal life, they might not accept him in other ways."

The President grinned. "I understand he's a very sexually active man."

"The word active," Johnston said, "doesn't begin to describe it."

"He was married, but his wife . . . well, she was killed," Fletcher said.

The President shook his head, but didn't say anything.

"I need your permission, Mister President, to instruct Admiral Kirkson to treat Admiral Boxer and the members of his crew as guests rather than prisoners," Fletcher said.

"Is that the way you think we should go?" the President asked.

"Absolutely. By treating him with kindness, we will indicate to the world at large that this Administration is not out for Boxer's blood. It will also signal court-martial to be very careful about what they are doing."

"Alright, send Admiral Kirkson whatever messages you think are necessary."

"What we could use right now is another war, like the one in the Persian Gulf a few years ago," Johnston commented. "That put almost everyone in the country on our side."

The President nodded, then in a wistful tone, said, "A good, little war comes down the pike only once in a couple of centuries . . . and it has already been fought and won."

"Right now, our first priority is to develop the Java strike as quickly as we can," Fletcher said.

"Absolutely," Johnston concurred.

"Well, gentlemen, I have another appointment in ten minutes," the President said, "and a formal dinner at seven."

Johnston, a heavyset man, who had played pro football, laughed, and said, "If that's your polite way, Mister President, of getting rid of us—"

"Getting rid of you," Fletcher said, matter-of-factly. "As for me, I'll be here for the next meeting, too."

Johnston stood, shook hands with the President and Fletcher, then said, "I'm out of here!"

The President waited for a few moments after the door was closed before he said, "That man has the 'lean and hungry look' of a potential candidate for this office."

"The look might be 'lean and hungry,' but he sure as hell isn't. He's a 'fat cat' if there ever was one," Fletcher said.

The President leaned back in his swivel chair, and drumming the fingers of his right hand on the desk, asked, "What is your personal assessment of this Boxer affair?"

"I have various opinions, or more precisely viewpoints," Fletcher said.

"Alright, I'm listening."

"Politically, it can sink you. The environmental issue will be big in your opponent's agenda," Fletcher said.

"Agreed," said the President with a nod.

"It would be equally politically unwise to interfere with the court-martial."

The President nodded, but did not speak.

"That puts you between the proverbial rock and a hard place."

"So?"

"You don't have much choice other than to remain on the sidelines," Fletcher said.

"That's not very reassuring," the President commented.

"It's the best I can do," Fletcher answered. "Unless, of course you want me to paint the world rosy for you."

With a wave of his hand, the President dismissed the idea, then said, "You couldn't do that even if you tried."

Fletcher smiled. "I don't do that."

"What about the man, Boxer?"

"Cool, calm, courageous and deadly, if he chooses to be," Fletcher said. "His men would follow him anywhere, any time. So would I if I were under his command. But he isn't everyman's 'cup of tea.' He has his enemies. Admiral Kirkson probably is one of those who hates Boxer's guts, and would probably keep him penned in the brig, if we hadn't interfered. Kirkson is by the book; Boxer doesn't believe the *book* exists."

"What about Boxer's relation with the Russian, Admiral Igor Borodine?" the President asked.

"A friendship forged by their many attempts to destroy each other. In a way, they are mirror images of one another. Borodine has all of the traits that Boxer has, but his emotional life is more stable. He has a wife and a child."

"What will his position be now that the Soviet Union no longer exists?"

Fletcher shrugged. "At the moment he's here as a naval attaché. But since his government has ceased to exist, well, everything is confused."

The President stood up, walked behind his chair, and looked at the Rose Garden, which was already beginning to show signs of the encroaching winter. "Drop a few veiled hints in the right places that my sympathies are with Boxer, but justice must have its day." He faced Fletcher. "That way I'll cover both sides of the street without having to commit to either."

"Yes, Mister President," Fletcher answered.

"And make sure that he is well treated wherever he goes," the President said.

"Absolutely, Mister President," Fletcher answered.

The President glanced at his calendar, then at the grandfather clock against the wall at the opposite side of the room. "I'm already ten minutes late for my next appointment," he said.

Within minutes, the winds strengthened and were blowing at eighty miles an hour, and gusting to one hundred and five.

"Give the order for the ships to turn into the wind," Kirkson shouted above the howling of the wind.

"Aye, aye, sir," Host answered.

Moments later, a junior officer reported, "The frigate *Warren* has lost rudder control."

"Holy Christ!" Kirkson exclaimed.

The WO reported, "Ship's surface radar out."

Kirkson looked at the scope. The screen was filled with snow.

Host returned. "Ship's executing your order, sir," he said.

Suddenly, the Klaxon screamed the signal for battle

26

stations. Then 1MC came on, "All hands, now hear this . . . Fire, in main hanger."

Kirkson peered down at the deck through the rain spattered window. The ship was already beginning to trail a plume of black smoke.

Just as he stepped away from the window, Host said, "COMM reports loss of radio contact with the *Warren*."

Kirkson's eyes went wide. Then in a low, almost threatening voice, he said, "Tell me that again, Commander, and be damn sure that you got it right."

Host stared straight at him. "COMM reports loss of radio contact with the frigate *Warren*," he repeated.

"Loss of radio contact," Kirkson echoed, and snapping his fingers, he added, "Just like that?"

"The *Warren* can't be raised, sir," Host said stiffly.

Before Kirkson could answer, two quick explosions rocked the ship. Flames shot out of the hole blown open in the aft section of the deck.

"Get me a damage and casualty report, Commander," Kirkson ordered.

"Aye, aye, sir," Host answered, and immediately went to the bank of phones.

Kirkson watched the flames. They leaped higher and higher, then suddenly dropped below the level of the deck, leaving only black smoke to pour out of the fissure.

"Fire under control . . . three dead, five suffering from burns and another ten from smoke inhalation. . . . Four jets damaged . . . two destroyed. And there was considerable damage to the hangar area."

27

Kirkson acknowledged the report with a nod, then he said, "Tell Captain Downs that I want a preliminary report of the accident on my desk. Relay that! He has more important things to do than write a report. There will be plenty of time for that. Now, we have to ride out this storm."

"Yes, sir," Host answered.

"That's a ship!" Boxer exclaimed, as he stared at the UWIS screen, where a three-dimensional image of an upside-down frigate, the *Warren*, was displayed.

"I don't fucking believe it!" Sarkis muttered. "It's sinking."

"No, it has already sunk," Boxer said. "It's just going to its final resting place." He glanced at the fathometer. The bottom was twelve thousand feet down. "They'll have a deep grave by any standard," he commented.

"Can you make out who she is?" Sarkis asked.

"No."

The dead ship was at the lower right of the UWIS screen.

Thinking aloud, Boxer assessed, "She probably was caught by a wave broadside, and went over."

"It's a helluva way to go!"

Boxer looked at him. "No matter which way you go, it's a helluva way to go." Then he added, "But the sea, like a woman in love, will have any man whenever she wants him."

Sarkis raised his eyebrows, but didn't say anything.

The dead ship slipped off the UWIS.

Boxer moved back to his chair in front of the master control computer and stretched. Watching the ship slowly descend to its deep grave, made him melancholy and introspective. His future had always seemed uncertain, but now it included the certainty of a court-martial, and the very real possibility of being given a prison sentence. That his career might end so ignobly was more than enough to make him reflect on his entire life. In many ways it seemed purposeless, though he realized that many men envied it. He might have felt more fulfilled by pursuing some other profession, one that would have allowed him to live a more normal kind of life with a wife and a family. Again, most men would envy his numerous affairs. But when they were over—often through no fault of his—he was left with nothing. . . .

Boxer pushed the melancholy thoughts back into that part of his brain where they would not hamper his ability to make command decisions. But they were there waiting to swoop back into his consciousness, acting as both the devourer and the carrion the moment he let them.

"Skipper, COMMO picked up a radio transmission ID'ing the lost ship as the frigate, *Warren,*" Sarkis reported.

Boxer shook his head.

"They never had a chance," Sarkis commented.

Boxer uttered a deep sigh, made an open gesture with his hands, and then ordered a surface weather check.

"Winds at eighty knots, gusting to ninety-five . . .

sea running at thirty-five feet, or more," Sarkis reported.

"We'll stay down," Boxer said, then he added, "Signal Admiral Kirkson that we will maintain our position relative to the *America*."

"Aye, aye, sir," Sarkis answered.

Chapter Three

On the flag bridge of the *America,* Admiral Kirkson received the message from the President with stone-faced fury. But being a better than average poker player, he knew that he still held a few good cards. After all, if Boxer hadn't insisted on *special treatment* for himself and his crew, the carrier group would have been underway, and out of the path of the typhoon. And the *Warren* would not have gone down with all hands. . . .

"Host?" Kirkson called.

"Yes, sir."

"Would you say that the delay caused by Admiral Boxer's demands for special treatment endangered the ships and men under my command?"

Host almost did a double take, and in the dim light of the bridge, he stared at Kirkson.

"Commander, did you hear my question?"

"Yes, sir."

"Well, do you have an answer?"

Weighing his words carefully, Host said, "I am not entirely sure what you are trying to establish.

But if it is a cause and effect relationship between Admiral Boxer's actions and the loss of the *Warren,* I don't think the relationship would be able to stand any sort of rigorous examination."

Kirkson squinted at him; that his intent had been so easily recognized and then obliterated did not please him. But there was nothing he could do about it . . . yet.

Tosenko paced the floor of his office, and having crossed it several times, stopped in front of a huge wall map of what had once been the USSR. Now it was a loose confederation of diverse countries without any direction, other than to survive. He was in exactly the same predicament: he wanted to survive. He *had* to survive.

He walked to the desk, took a Cuban cigar out of the teakwood humidor, and before starting to pace again, cut one end of the cigar and lit the other. The cigar tasted good, and made him think of the other pleasures of life: beautiful women, exquisite-tasting wines, and *haute cuisine*. In the years he had been connected with Stempler, he had enjoyed all of them. But he knew that unless he could do what Eric Von wanted him to, he'd be finished. He'd lose everything, including his mistress, Ellen Rogers.

Tosenko realized that he'd have to somehow bribe the men on the court-martial with money. Lots of it could buy anything, even a United States naval officer.

32

He moved to the window, and looked out on to the upper bay, where the Statue of Liberty was located. Two Staten Island ferries were plowing through the wind ruffled waters. One going to the island, the other coming from it. Then he saw it, lying low in the water, dark and menacing. It was one of the *John Adams* class of ballistic missile submarines, a monster of its kind. Some five hundred feet in length, a beam of sixty feet. With its missiles equipped with MIRV warheads it could destroy every major city on each of the five continents.

Tosenko went to his desk, opened the bottom drawer and took out a pair of high-powered, infra-red binoculars. Returning to the window, he trained the glasses on the slowly moving submarine.

The men on the sail were clearly visible.

For several moments, Tosenko studied the boat. Then, like a character in a cartoon, he felt the sudden flash of an idea light up his entire brain. He returned to his desk, and dialed Stempler's private number.

The phone rang three times before Stempler picked it up.

Without any preliminaries, Tosenko said, "A submarine would be the answer to all our problems . . . a *Volga* class boat."

"Yes, I had something similar in mind," Stempler answered.

"As soon as this business with Boxer is wrapped up, I'll see if something can be arranged."

"Good, very good," Stempler said.

Tosenko was about to wish Eric Von Stempler well on his vacation, but he had already clicked off.

"All hands, now hear this . . . all hands, now hear this . . . standby," Sarkis announced over the 1MC. Then, he nodded to Boxer.

Boxer activated his 1MC mike, and said, "This is the captain speaking. In a short while we will be surfacing, and we will be under the jurisdiction of the Marine boarding party. This crew will be taken aboard the *America,* and a new crew will operate this boat.

"But before that happens I want to thank everyone for being with me on this mission. What we have done is more important than all of the other missions that we previously had shared. But all of you know that.

"All I can do now is wish you good luck . . ." He paused, then said, "All hands, stand by to surface . . . surface." Then he sounded the Klaxon.

The instant the helicopter touched down on the *America's* flight deck, the media crews rushed forward. Their high intensity lights placed a circle of white light on the chopper's door.

Kirkson would have placed an armed guard around the copter the moment it landed, but the message from the President made him back away from doing it. Instead, he absented himself from the events that were taking place on the flight deck, and remained on the flag bridge.

The door of the chopper opened, and Boxer stepped out. Immediately there was a burst of applause from deck crew, and the media people.

Microphones were shoved in front of Boxer, but he refused to say anything. His XO, Commander Sarkis, also refused to speak.

"You think you've got it made, Mister. But you better think again," Kirkson said to himself.

The group on the deck dispersed, and Boxer and Sarkis vanished inside the ship's island.

"All hands, now hear this. . . . Prepare to get underway . . . prepare to get underway," a disembodied voice announced over the 1MC.

Kirkson nodded, and Host repeated the command to the men on the flag bridge.

The dinner was held in Captain Downs's quarters. Boxer sat at the captain's right, next to him was Sarkis. Thomas Crieder was on Downs's left, and next to him sat Carol Benson. The other places at the table were occupied by the senior officers of ship's company, and its air wing.

"Unofficially, I want to congratulate you for doing what had to be done," Downs said.

"And unofficially, I accept your congratulations," Boxer answered.

"You have enough public support back home to

beat the rap," Crieder said, as a steward served the main course of roast beef, french fries, and carrots and peas.

"Maybe in a civilian court, but a Navy court-martial is different," Boxer answered politely.

"I think our news program can generate enough mail to have your court members dismiss the charges," Carol Benson said.

Boxer looked at her.

"If you committed a crime, it was to right a wrong," she continued.

"I don't think the Navy will look at it that way," Boxer said, his eyes focused on her. She was a tall woman, with a svelte figure, and full, high breasts. She had red hair, which she wore shoulder length. Her eyes were blue, and full of flashing light. A scattering of freckles dotted the bridge of her nose and cheeks.

"A court-martial is very serious," Downs said.

Boxer nodded.

"Public opinion is a very powerful weapon," Crieder commented. "If the Navy wants a fight, that's just what the media will give them."

"To the good fight!" Carol Benson toasted, standing up and raising her glass of water.

Everyone stood up, raised their glasses and echoed Carol's words.

Kirkson paced the width of his office; it was almost more than he could bear that the ship's captain and his senior officers were having a celebration dinner to honor Boxer.

Kirkson came from three generations of Navy and there was no chance that he was going to let this pirate get away from him. Boxer had been an object of loathing for him prior to this present situation. When Kirkson had been an instructor at the Academy, Boxer had been involved in naval misadventures across the oceans of the world. Any of them would have been enough to give a bad name to the Navy. For Kirkson that was the equivalent of spitting in the face of the Pope.

Kirkson was also impatient and he had to force himself to wait. There would be time to get Boxer at the court-martial. After all, it was not going to be a civilian trial. It was going to be a Navy show and Kirkson knew how to handle those. The man *is* a pirate, for Christ's sake, he thought. Deep in his heart, he felt that the loss of the frigate was actually his responsibility, but his need for a "cover your ass" factor had forced him to fly the idea of Boxer being responsible. He determined that if there were nothing else he could do, he could make the arrival of the crew of the hijacked SSN-S1 back in the United States as uncomfortable and ugly as possible.

He paced back to his desk and stabbed a button.

"Yes, Admiral?" His yeoman snapped.

"Get me the commander of the Marine detachment and the sergeant at arms in the brig."

"Aye, aye, sir."

Let's see if the manacles are in working order? he
thought.

Had he been an admiral in the eighteenth century, he would have been considering keelhauling.
But, alas, he thought, the Navy had softened.

Chapter Four

Six thousand miles to the south southwest, east of the straits of Selat Sundra, and at the very edge of the precipice that was the Java trench, Elltyn Van der Meer mopped his brow as he squinted at the side scanning sonar picture of his drilling posture. The SDS mounted sonar created a fairly detailed, echo-induced picture of the deep and the strange position which the *Deep Six* held relative to the drilling position of the rig on the surface and the waiting black gold of the Java strike below. The drilling position was dangerous and unique. A seafloor crawling rig was all that could have been used to manage to penetrate perhaps the largest untapped pool of light sweet crude on the planet. Whatever she was, the rig had to be moveable, pressure resistant, and self-contained at multiple ton per square inch pressures at a depth of nearly a thousand feet. The *Deep Six* was perfect for the job. Unfortunately for Elltyn and the Halcyon Oil development A.G. of Amsterdam, there were other deep drilling rigs on station at the edge of the trench as well as more on the way from the Seven Sisters and all of the other oil development lash-ups in the world.

Besides being one of the largest strikes in the world, it was perhaps the most dangerously positioned. The Java Deep, like the Cayman Deep and others, was not far from land. Indeed, she was too close. The drilling operation which fed pipe and bits from the surface where support ships were sea anchored relied on the *Deep Six* to direct the bit and underwater length of flex drilling pipe directly into the upper strata of the oil chamber. She was to do this while taking core samples every few minutes. These were designed to insure that she came up with crude and not natural gas which was being saved to pump up the deeper reserves.

As drilling chief on the rig, Elltyn had more than twenty years of experience from Saudi wells, to the North Sea and the American Gulf of Mexico. He could move a sea bottom rig anywhere, but even he had to admit that the elbow room here was close to nonexistent. Furthermore, his crew had been on the rig for three weeks working grueling twelve hour days. The twenty-seven men were clearly ready for a day or two leave in the fleshpots of Jakarta or north to Singapore, and moving the *Deep Six* got a bit sticky.

"Skipper?" Sonarman Van Kleek called in guttural Dutch.

"Ja?" Elltyn grunted.

"I have a sonar target coming up from the trench."

40

"Up?"

"Yes, sir. Up. Wait. Now, there are two."

"Can you say which type?" Elltyn asked with a slight edge in his voice. Nothing was supposed to be coming from the trench.

"Hard to say, sir. The last time I saw this echo was at sea during anti-sub . . . oh shit!"

"What is it? Van Kleek! What the fuck is it?"

Van Kleek's eyes were riveted to the screen. The two targets were closing on the *Deep Six* and they were splitting up. One of them was heading to the stern of the rig and one was coming in abeam. It was a classic attack pattern. It went back to fighter aircraft in World War Two.

"Skipper, I don't like this."

Elltyn looked to the screen and he could understand the genesis of Van Kleek's fear.

"See if you can raise them on the 'Granny.' "

Underwater radio contact had always been the bane of undersea operations. The "Granny" was the answer to that. She was an extremely low frequency radio device to be used by submarines in cases of emergency. By boosting the signal, she could make herself heard to the vessels that approached.

Elltyn grabbed the mike before Van Kleek could; the craft were coming quite close at what could only be considerable speed underwater.

"Unidentified craft," he shouted in imperfect English. "We are the *Deep Six* of the Halcyon Oil Company drilling in our legally leased area. State your business."

There was no answer.

Elltyn called out the hail again.

Nothing.

One of the craft which Elltyn had determined to be minisubs had moved closer to the blind stern of the rig and the other was close to the small, two inch quartz port that Elltyn could peer through.

"Sound the collision alarm," he snapped to Van Kleek. "Close all watertight doors and assemble all off-duty crew in the ER-One."

"Roger," Van Kleek barked and he slammed his fist into a broad red mushroom of a button that occupied a prominent place in the control panel.

In the distance red and yellow lights started to flash and a Klaxon screamed twice a second.

The crew of the *Deep Six* scrambled in the direction of their emergency stations. Elltyn had been scrupulous in drilling them several times a week and included pay bonuses for speedy reaction time.

No crew member was stationed more than a thirty second run from a specified emergency station and all such stations were connected to ER-One; the rig's escape pod. Actually the device was an unbelievably cramped small sub compressed with the right number of atmospheres and flooded with the correct heli-ox mixtures. It was attached to the surface mother ship with an umbilicus and a series of one-inch steel cables that could decompress the chamber and raise it to the surface over an eighteen hour period.

"Son of a bitch," Van Kleek gasped. "The one on

the beam has fired something." He looked from the monitor and snapped on the speaker that flooded the control room with the sonar clutter that the on-board computer was sorting out.

Elltyn looked at the smaller man at the console. "What is that? I can't make that out?"

Van Kleek went gray. The sound he was picking out from the clutter was one that he remembered from the days when he had been a sonar operator for the Dutch Navy. "High-speed screw. It's a torpedo, Skipper."

Elltyn shook his head. He did not doubt his subordinate for a second. *Why* was the question that was flashing into his mind. The other question was *how?* How will my crew survive?

"Target analysis. High speed rotation indicates an Oldynsiav Mark XX wire guided long-range torpedo with a warhead capacity of one ton of high explosive . . ." The computer's female voice was annoyingly calm.

"Time to impact?" Elltyn asked, his tone grim.

"Just over a minute," Van Kleek answered.

"Alert the surface."

As Van Kleek was giving the bad news to the mother ship on the surface, Elltyn was hitting the intercom to speak to the crew.

"This is Elltyn. We are in the process of being attacked by two small subs. They are in attack positions now and have fired a torpedo. You have just over a minute until impact. All hands get into the ER-One and hold for further orders. Do not dog the hatch. I will be last in. Jump to it."

"Forty-five seconds," Van Kleek yelled. "Topside knows. They are calling the Indonesian authorities. Why would anybody . . . ?"

"Get to the ER-One. I'm going to try to evade."

"You can't evade, Skipper. They can steer."

"Get into the ER-One, anyway. Perhaps there is a chance we can be talked out of this."

Van Kleek took a fast look at the monitor. "Thirty or so. Come with me, Skipper." Elltyn watched as the torpedo started to accelerate. "Maybe you're right. . . ." He was out of his seat and moving now. "Doesn't look like they're the kind to be convinced of anything."

Both men started running in the direction of the ER-One. As they dashed from the control room, Elltyn pressed a button that closed the final WTD that separated the outer surface of the control room from the sea and the corridor they were entering.

They dashed ten yards down the steel corridor and swung to the right. Ahead of them, some thirty feet distant, was the ER-One. Its hatch was open and crew members crowded inside. Many had jammed at the door and now peered out from the inside yelling for the skipper and his sonarman to run.

Five hundred yards below a hand moved a control slide and the tiny line that spun out to the Oldynsiav Mark XX sent a pulse of energy and the torpedo leapt ahead, cutting the impact time by half.

Elltyn and Van Kleek were still ten feet from the

hatch when the torpedo impacted on the control room behind them.

The blast had the effect of a close aboard hit on a sub by a depth charge. The explosion was followed by what seemed an implosion. A gash was ripped in the control room and the chamber filled with twenty-eight degree seawater in a matter of seconds. As the cold sea hit the electronics of the controls, electricity arced in all directions blowing circuit breakers and throwing the heating and electric power to the *Deep Six* out of commission.

Elltyn and Van Kleek were thrown from their feet to the steel plates of the floor as the control room exploded behind them. The watertight door that had just been closed was partially breached and seawater started to flood the corridor.

As the two of them got to their feet, they were knee-deep in frigid seawater that hit them like thousands of knife blades. They were within an arm's reach of the hatch when the water was starting to play around their hips. Inside the ER-One the crew was screaming for them to get inside. In another second or two it would become impossible to close the hatch and they would drown along with the two who were attempting to enter through the hatch.

A tide of water swept Elltyn and Van Kleek into the chamber, a force of water equal to the combined muscle strength of eight or ten men.

It took them only five seconds to dog the hatch shut but when the crew were finished they were soaking wet in freezing water and totally spent.

Twenty-nine men were now jammed in the ER-One which was filled waist deep with frigid water.

Elltyn held tight to a stanchion as he shouted orders.

"Build the air pressure and activate the pumps. We're too heavy to get topside with all this water."

It took more time than they expected to pump the ER-One dry and then to decompress properly to get the crew to the surface.

When Elltyn stepped gingerly from the ER-One he was informed that the *Deep Six* was totally useless as far as surveillance robots could determine. And, there was more.

Three other floor drilling rigs in the Java Strike had been hit in the same way. Someone wanted the Java Strike out of commission.

In the immense CIA Langley complex, careful computer analysis was underway on a mosaic of the crippled operations in the Java strike. Harry T. Olsen, CIA Director, peered glumly at the satellite mosaics that had been placed on his desk as a part of the morning briefing. He looked up to the briefer, Emmett Cosgrove, a young man from the Far Eastern desk who he remembered as extremely bright.

"How many, Emmett?"

"In total, there were three rigs attacked. One from Shell, another from Halcyon, and a third from British North Sea, sir."

"Were they all destroyed?"

"Not all, sir. But the drilling operations there will be held up for awhile. At the same time, OPEC has raised its prices to forty-two dollars a barrel. That's an all-time high."

"I know," Olsen muttered. He knew he was going to have to tell the President and he was not happy about it. The price of oil in an election year that already sported a serious contender and a weak economy was not something that the President was going to want to hear about. "Is there a line on what did all of this?"

"Not much, sir. The commander of the *Deep Six* a Dutchman named . . ." He paused and consulted his notes. "Van der Meer. Yes, Elltyn Van der Meer says he tracked what appeared to be two minisubs and one or both of them fired homing torpedoes into him. He said that if they can get the rig back to the surface, there's a chance that they can get a recording of the computer data."

"Sabotage then?"

"It would seem so, sir."

"Goddamn towel heads," Olsen grumbled. "Forty-two dollars a barrel. Jesus."

Aboard the *America*, Boxer and Sarkis had spent the better part of a week in the brig and literally in chains. He looked up to see Marine Captain Geron, the man whose life he'd saved only days before.

"I'm sorry about all this, Admiral," the young man said. Boxer watched as his eyes moved to the waist manacles and the hand and leg irons that both he and Sarkis sported.

"I didn't believe it when the admiral ordered these. Captain Downs had no choice. I'm sure you know about that, Admiral?"

"Don't worry about it, son. We sure managed to get the son of a bitch pissed, though, didn't we?"

Geron grinned broadly. "You sure did, sir. I thought the old man was going to wet his pants when the captain ordered up that formal dinner."

The young marine looked around to see if there were any eavesdroppers. There were none.

"I ordered the Marine detach to take off the shackles at night. The odds are that the admiral wouldn't come down to gloat then."

"I think we're safe. Kirkson was here yesterday to read me the penalties for piracy. I told him he should retire. He loved that."

Sarkis rattled his manacles in the corner of the cell. "I'd like to retire him."

"So would I, Sarkis," Boxer chimed in. "So would I."

Boxer turned to the young Marine captain. "Son, be real careful of that son of a bitch. He would take delight in shortening the career of a young officer . . . especially a Marine officer." Boxer paused for a second as if to feel the movement of the deck beneath his feet.

"We have to be close."

"Close?"

"To land. That's a ground swell I feel. I expect

Norfolk."

"That's right, sir."

"And in the dead of night?"

"Correct, sir."

"That fits. I expect he wants to get us off the ship in irons also."

"I'm not sure about that, Admiral, but I know he is having a hell of a time with that lady reporter . . . ah Miss Benson? Well, she's hitting him with everything from the Freedom of Information Act to the First Amendment and I think everything in between. He doesn't even go near the officers' ward room now. He has all of his meals and coffee in his sea cabin and he's told the men in my detachment to prevent her from seeing him. Yup, she sure has the old man pissed."

"Not pissed enough," Sarkis chirped, from the corner of the cell.

Boxer laughed despite the fact that the chains were chafing his wrists and ankles. The laugh ended abruptly and he grew serious. "Has she managed to file a story anywhere?"

"I don't really know, sir. I do know that they plan to fly you in from the *America* when we get close, which we are now. I expect they want to whisk you past the press. They might do it, too. Miss Benson has been denied the communications room facilities. There is a good chance no one on the outside knows when you and your crew will be coming in."

"No one has allowed me to see the crew. Are they

all right?"

"As well as can be expected in the brig, sir. They're griping but I've given my men instructions to not tolerate any harassment of them. After all, these are your crewmen; you and they saved a dozen of my men's lives. No way they would be harassed."

Boxer felt relieved about his men but he knew that the real problems he was going to face were on shore. He was sure that the Navy would not focus on his crew. He would be the target . . . he would be the *pirate*. He would only have a few hours to wait.

Carol Benson stood with Tom Crieder on the bow of the carrier and looked shoreward into the warm spring night.

"That's Norfolk, isn't it?" she asked.

"Yup," Crieder answered. "And there's a good chance that Kirkson will keep us cruising in circles out here until he manages to transport Boxer on shore by chopper in the dead of night. No radio, no press. And, by the time we get to shore, there's a good chance that they will be ensconced in cells in Norfolk Naval Prison and held incommunicado."

"How can Kirkson get away with that?" Carol snapped with a clear edge to her voice.

"He is an admiral commanding a flotilla at sea, babe. That's how. I spent four years in the Navy once upon a time. Part of it was in the South China Sea . . . place called Yankee Station. A man in

Kirkson's place can damn near do what he wants. The only thing he has to worry about is the publicity you'll give him. If he can prevent that, there's a chance he can make it work. And as far as I can see, he's effectively *prevented* both us from communicating."

He looked at her and there was a twinkle in her eye and the hint of a smile curled her lips. "Okay, Carol. I must be missing something. What exactly swept past me?"

"Not a lot, Tom. Just . . . enough. All I have to do is wait until I can get in range of my cell."

"They're not going to put you in a cell, babe. They're after Boxer, remember."

She responded with a deep and hearty laugh. Her breasts pushed against the gray khaki work shirt she wore, and she started to unbutton it, revealing a black bra underneath. Tom, caught totally unaware, gawked and looked around for a second. He wanted to believe it was for his benefit, but he was somehow sure it was not.

"Here it is, Tom. This will foil the good admiral. So much for the absolute power of a ship's master at sea and all that nautical horse shit."

She pulled from the insides of the loose khaki shirt a cellular phone. "That's the cell, I mean, Tom. And, there is a good chance that we will be in range within a mile or two. If we can manage to get in range before they ship Boxer and company to shore, I can have everyone on God's green earth down on the helipad."

Recovering his composure, Crieder shook his head.

"Kirkson will shit, won't he?" Carol Benson smiled broadly and nodded. She was counting the minutes as the task force came closer to Norfolk and the range of her satellite cell.

It was three in the morning when Boxer and the others were awakened by a Klaxon horn blaring in the brig. Apparently it was something normally used to awaken sleeping prisoners, though Boxer thought it sounded more like a collision alarm. After a minute of din, the Klaxon stopped and Kirkson, along with a reluctant Downs, came into the brig. They were followed by a Marine escort armed with M-18s and wearing their blue and scarlet dress uniform that was a tribute to Geron's spit and polish leadership. "The Marine detachment will escort the prisoners to the embarkation point." Kirkson's voice had a little more edge than normal to it. Boxer couldn't be sure what was with the man . . . did he think they were going to try to escape?

"Aye, aye, sir," Captain Geron snapped. He moved into position to open the cell.

Boxer had not been allowed to shave for several days and Sarkis was in the same situation. Boxer had intended to say nothing to Kirkson when he saw him again. But, the man's demeanor forced him to open his mouth.

"Be advised, Admiral, I am going to bring charges against you personally for the mistreatment my crew and I have received at your direct orders."

"You're a pirate, Boxer, and you have no grounds."

"I am a prisoner, sir . . . not yet convicted of anything. There are certain rights I have been denied. NR 600-24, paragraph twenty, states that prisoners are allowed . . . indeed, *required* to have a health and welfare visit from a physician on a daily basis when they are manacled or in such incarceration as we. We have received no such visits."

The last thing that Kirkson expected was that Boxer, long known to be the absolute bane of Naval regulations, would have turned out to be such a studious brig lawyer.

Kirkson blinked before responding. "I won't have to worry about that until after your court-martial, Mister. Then, you will have no civil rights and no case. Move them out, Lieutenant Geron."

The marine officer stepped forward. No one was surprised at his being demoted a rank. All "captains" became "Lieutenant" on shipboard. The ship could have only one "real" captain.

It only took a second for Boxer to see that Sarkis and the crewmen were not coming with him. He stopped the chain-shrouded parade down the companionway and turned back to Kirkson.

"Where are they being sent, Kirkson? Are they being kept here? You can't keep them incommunicado forever, you know."

"It's none of your fucking business, pirate. Now, march."

On the flight deck, Boxer was surprised to see that it was nighttime. He had lost track of the exact time of day in the brig where there were no portholes. It seemed right, he thought. Middle of the night. There was a chance that the others, Sarkis included, might be shipped to other bases . . . perhaps Philadelphia, where they would be taken off also in the middle of the night.

How the hell much information got out? He could only wonder and hope that the wire services had managed to pick up the story. They were perhaps his only hope. He distantly remembered studying at Annapolis the life of General Billy Mitchell. When the Army had court-martialed Mitchell, they had held the trial in an old Army warehouse at Fort Myers, as far from the mainstream as they could get. Mitchell had been drummed out for suggesting that air power and the carrier along with the submarine would someday be the backbone of the Navy. He had also suggested that the next war would be with the Japanese, as they had the most to gain from the conquest of the Pacific.

Not far off on the flight deck the Sea Stallion helicopter was slowly turning its blades, the pilot patiently waiting for his passengers.

Boxer, hobbled by the chains, managed to make decent progress in the direction of the helicopter. As he came close, he looked back toward the island. Sure enough Kirkson was standing on the bridge watching silently. But, below him, on the flight deck standing next to an open hatch was Carol Benson. Boxer could feel his mouth water and his groin tingle. She waved and Boxer thought he saw her blow him a kiss.

They clambered on the Sea Stallion and just before the doors were swung closed, Captain Downs hopped aboard. He waited until they were airborne before he came to Boxer and cupped a hand to his ear so no one could hear.

"I am sure you know none of this . . . the chains and stuff, was my doing. There are times when I think Admiral Charles Laughton back there belongs in the nineteenth century."

"Not to worry," Boxer grinned. "A man like that is his own worst enemy. If you're worried about your fitness report, there are good odds that the Navy Department doesn't fitness reports such a man hands in literally."

"He'll be in the Huey that's trailing us to the dock. We'll be met there by a car and you'll be taken to the Norfolk brig where they'll present the formal charges." He shook his head. "You know I think this whole thing sucks, Admiral."

"You are not the Lone Ranger, son. What about Sarkis and the rest of the crew?"

"They're going to wait on them. It seems that Admiral Kirkson is determined to make an example of you, personally. And, the rest of them can wait until they evaluate what percentage of them were conspirators and what percentage of them were simply

55

obeying orders. Knowing the old man, though, he'll want every ass hanging from the yardarm."

"The perils of being a rebel," Boxer said. "When you're down, all of the people who were too chicken-shit to do what you've done kick you in the *cojones*. Like a turkey in the barnyard."

The Sea Stallion swung into the Norfolk Navy Base airspace and followed the direction of the Air Control Officer, moving to a remote corner of the base where she touched down. Before the ground crew had a chance to run out on the helipad and open the hatch, the second bird touched down only a dozen yards away. It was the Huey carrying Kirkson.

The admiral wanted to be the first to see Boxer's face now that he was only hours from being charged. He un-dogged the hatch and slid the huge Huey door back.

The glare of lights shattered his night vision and for a second or two he stood in the hatchway blinking owl-like. As the spinning rotors slowed and the deafening whine decreased, and as Kirkson's night vision started to return, he could see them. A sea of them . . . a host of humanity with tape recorders and portapacks and notebooks.

"Reporters! Fuck!" he slowly mouthed.

They were locusts, attempting to swarm at the helicopter and restrained by a cordon of Marine guards.

How the hell did they know?

As he watched in horror, the Sea Stallion's hatch

opened a few yards away and the Marine guard led the shackled Boxer out. He looked gray and grizzled . . . an innocent man terribly wronged, fleeing the gallows, like the hero of *Les Misérables*.

Reporters, prevented from getting close, yelled questions at him and, though he could not exactly hear the words because of the helicopter noise, he smiled in the direction of the cameras and lights raising his manacled hands in an overhead Victory handclasp.

Chained hands held aloft and a smile on Boxer's grizzled face were on the cover of nearly every American daily the next day. It would be a week later when the same image, carefully turned into a collage, would grace the cover of *Time* and *Newsweek*. Their headlines bore sinister warnings about nuclear power and the disposal of waste. *The Christian Science Monitor* said "The Hot Spot Is A Test Case."

Kirkson watched all of this start to happen with the air of a man watching his mother-in-law drive off a cliff in his new Mercedes.

Reporters swirled on Boxer's periphery screaming questions. One reporter managed to break through the thin and overworked Marine line and pushed a mike into Boxer's face. "Admiral, is it true that you buried the worst nuclear contamination area in the world?"

Boxer kept moving in the direction of the waiting gray staff car but slowed to answer the question. The marines did nothing to stop the reporter. That would have been the ultimate calamity and they knew it: slam an M-18 butt into the chest of a reporter while his colleagues get the whole thing on take. It would hit the media like the L.A. police beating tape had some years before.

Boxer managed a smile. "They tell me it was the largest. All I know is that I'm being tried for piracy because of the incident and I am going to have to fight for my life and the lives of my crew."

"*Did* you commit an act of piracy, Admiral?"

Boxer could not resist the chance to grandstand. Odds were that this would be the last press exposure he could get before the upcoming court-martial.

"What I did was make an attempt to save the environment from being ravaged by the contamination born of nuclear waste. It was more an attempt to clean the planet than anything else. After all, it was private interests that dumped that material there in the first place and they were paid a huge sum by various companies and . . ." Boxer smiled after a brief pause. ". . . perhaps even nations who ordered the dumping in the first place."

One of the guards mistakenly stepped between the cameraman who was shooting footage of Boxer's answer and the admiral. The crowd of newsmen and women thought it was an attempt to keep Boxer from answering the question. There were boos and catcalls from the assembled news crews and shouts of "Let him talk," and "Fascist!" rang from the crowd.

The marine scurried out of the way. He was aware of what he had done and was making a real effort at suddenly looking invisible.

Taking advantage of the moment, Boxer raised his chained hands in the air and shouted to the jungle of assembled reporters and cameras.

"This is the reward for trying to heal a sick planet!"

There were shouts and cheers.

It was at this unfortunate moment that the livid Admiral Kirkson stepped out of his helicopter.

"You soldiers move the prisoner to the car. This is *not* a press conference. And you . . ." He turned to Boxer and his face was the color of wild strawberries. He snarled barely loud enough for Boxer to hear.

"You are a disgrace to the uniform you wear and the one that I hope you will not wear for much longer. I forbid you to speak."

Boxer, who had lowered his chained hands to his sides, raised them again to the sky so that all the cameras could catch them.

"The good admiral says I am a disgrace to the uniform for caving in the worst nuclear waste area on the planet. I wonder how connected he might be to the interests that placed the waste there in the first place."

It was a low blow and Boxer knew it. He was sure that there wasn't a chance in a million that Kirkson was connected to the interests that created the hot zone. But in a sense, it was just punishment for Kirkson had been such an ass to place Boxer in irons for the journey home.

As Boxer was being moved off in the direction of

the gray staff car, he could hear shouted questions bombarding Kirkson.

"What exactly is your connection to the hot zone incident, Admiral?"

"By whose orders . . . ?"

Boxer grinned. Kirkson would be an hour shaking loose of the news hounds and when he did he would have left a trail of "no comments," in his wake. There was nothing they liked more than a "no comment," because it allowed them to speculate and slant. And, that was something they were starting to do in favor of Boxer, the poor chained victim.

As he slid into the backseat of the staff car, the small victory over the buffoon Kirkson was starting to ring hollow in his ears. Beating Kirkson was like beating your grandmother at ice hockey.

Now he was going to have to fight the battle of his life . . . for his life. He was going to be tried for piracy. If he was found guilty, the mandatory sentence was death by hanging.

Chapter Five

Von Stempler looked at the television report from the Dutch East Indies and smiled for a second before the smile turned to a frown. There were other things that had to be checked. He pressed the button that direct dialed Tosenko and automatically started a scrambler. Tosenko answered on the first ring.

"Yes, sir?"

"I'm watching an account of the damage in the Java strike. Is there a chance that any of it can be traced to us? Have we totally covered our tracks?"

"No question. *Krieg* is doing fine. I hired the best of the new generation of mercs. Many of them are from what had been the Soviet fleet. A number have degrees in engineering. All of them have combat experience."

"And of the twelve rigs how many have been incapacitated?" Eric Von asked.

"One totally destroyed on the ocean floor. A second is severely damaged and has been pulled back to the surface. A third has been slightly damaged in an attack."

"Was that attack a failure?"

"No, sir," Tosenko answered. He wanted to admit nothing like failure to a man of Eric Von's stature. "They are aware by now that the attacks are coming from submarines, specifically launched from a mother craft deep in the trench. A number of the companies involved are hiring security forces who are employing fairly sophisticated surveillance hardware. The third . . . a Gelsen Oil Company rig managed to get a good active sonar fix on the two mini's before they could launch the torps. They did some damage with a conventional torpedo but the guided ones were too dangerous to use under those conditions. I didn't want to compromise the entire operation. I'm sure you understand, sir."

Von Stempler paused for a second and nodded slightly. Tosenko was right. It was better to be more concerned with security than anything else. Besides, there were too many rigs operational out there, anyway.

Von Stempler looked at the screens that monitored the London, Zurich, Bombay, and Tokyo markets. Wall Street was not open yet but the other markets in the world had managed to push the oil prices to thirty-five dollars a barrel with the last report of damage to a rig. It was about where he wanted the price . . . for now. But, in the near future he could see it topping at something in the range of fifty dollars a barrel. It would be at about that time that the oil producing governments of the world would be in utter chaos and many of them would fall. Their stock position would be precipitous. His financial interests would be able to acquire companies with ease. It made the late eighties and the rage of leveraged buy outs look like child's play. But, the late eighties did not have Von Stempler, he thought. Eric Von will show them.

"Sir?"

"What?"

It was Tosenko. He had been holding the phone patiently while Von Stempler had been in the midst of a money-fed reverie.

"Sir, with your permission, I am going to attempt to coordinate two attacks on two rigs at the same time. I can move the subs faster if they are alone, and there is a chance that the new pattern won't be seen by the security forces. I think we should carry out the operation soon. If all twelve of the rigs are going to be dumped, we had better think of things being completed in the next month. If we carry things out further than that, there is a chance that we can get found out."

"Very well. Speed things up a bit. But, I don't want *all* of the rigs to go at once. I want to do some manipulating in the market before they're all gone. You are also aware of what has to happen to the crews and the others when *Krieg* is completed?"

There was a momentary pause before Tosenko replied. When he did there was a small hitch in his voice, "Y-yes, sir."

Von Stempler knew well that erasing his tracks meant "removing" all of the mercs who had manned the subs. This was a detail that Tosenko was not in favor of . . . something that, indeed, he loathed. It was a matter over which Tosenko was going to have to wrestle with his conscience. He had to convince himself it was the best way to keep World Waste Disposal from exposure.

Von Stempler looked at the screen and the stock prices. "I think the next target should be Royal Dutch Shell, Arkady. See to it."

"Yes, sir."

Boxer paced the small cell as if it were the conning tower of a sub in a storm. There were no windows in the brig and few amenities. A stainless steel "head" stood in the corner next to a small sink. A swing down bunk with a two-inch mattress over steel slats hung from the far wall. There was a chair and a desk; little more could fit in a cell a mere nine by seven feet. A normal man might have started to feel claustrophobic but not Boxer. He had spent too much time as a submariner. He had been in World War Two *Guppy* class boats where everything was cheek by jowl. That was long before the enormous size of the *Trident* class boats had made the submariner's life more luxurious. Still, he was glad to occasionally get free of the cell. He had spent twenty-three hours a day "locked down" in it with two hours of exercise in the enclosed prison yard as the highlight of the twenty-four hour period. He had seen none of his shipmates while he was in the yard nor at any other time. The practice of removing him from his cell when there was no one else in sight reminded him of the treatment of "about-to-be-brainwashed" prisoners in the KGB's old Lubianka. It was meant to disorient a man. Well, Boxer thought, they won't do that to me.

He'd been visited by a Navy judge advocate-type who had informed him of the charges against him and told him that the trial would take over six months for the Navy to prepare. He thought it was preposterous. Why was there no chance for bail? If nothing else, Boxer couldn't imagine not getting laid for that long a time.

"Prisoner Boxer?"

Boxer turned at the cell door and saw a Marine guard standing there.

"Yes?" He had a little trouble not being called Admiral. But, that was the way things went in the brig.

"What is it, son?"

"You have a visitor."

"That's nice to hear. I thought I wasn't allowed them?"

"This relates to your defense. Visits from defense personnel, lawyers and such, are permitted to visit at any time."

The door of the cell electronically slipped from its latch and slipped to the side. The Lance Corporal, Boxer noticed the guard's rank, moved to the side so that when Boxer stepped from the cell he would turn in the direction of the end of the cell bay and have the guard behind him. It was a safety factor. The thought of escape had fleetingly crossed Boxer's mind when he had first arrived and he had played with the idea. The odds were too great, though. The act itself would add more charges to the list that already was headed by piracy.

Boxer turned the corner into the visitor's area that was a series of phone booths with glass partitions between the phone speakers. The marine turned him into one of the booths and he could see the somber face of Admiral Stark on the other side.

They had known one another for perhaps a quarter of a century; Stark the senior at the Academy half a dozen years before Boxer was a middie. They had served together for more years than either wanted to admit and Boxer was sure glad to see the craggy old face of the retired admiral.

"You look like three-day-old dog shit," Stark barked into the phone.

Boxer managed a smile. "I'd like to return the compliment but you look actually pretty good. Like to shake your hand, Tom. But, I've never been in the brig before."

Stark grew serious. "This is a huge mess, and it looks like the Navy is of two minds about it." His voice was barely above a whisper into the mouth piece on the phone. He was sure that there was a good chance that the conversation was being recorded but it didn't matter. He had to get a lot of information to Boxer in a hurry.

"You have a lot of friends on the outside, Jack. Perhaps more than you know. That grandstand thing you did with the media when they brought you ashore was something that will not soon be forgotten. The problem is that the Navy won't forget it in the same way that our friends won't. They're going to try to fry your ass real good."

"What about the crew?" Boxer interrupted.

Stark shook his head reassuringly. "They don't have it in for them as much as they do for you. Even Sarkis is basically off the hook. At least that's as far as I see it. No. You're the target because you are the symbol of resistance as far as the Navy is concerned. But, like I say, you have friends. Among them is a contingent from the United Nations."

"You don't mean *The* United Nations, Tom."

"I sure as shit do. There are a large number of countries that have fishing fleets that work in those waters. What you managed to do in demolishing the hot zone gave them a warning about the places that their fleets work. The lives of the crews of all of those fishing boats were in danger every time they went out. And, there is always the scenario of them selling contaminated fish to their markets and not knowing it. The lawsuits would be in the billions. No, you've got friends out there.

"What I came to talk about was your defense. The evidence that you actually did pirate the SSN-S1 is overwhelming. What we have to do is attack from the environmental view. Crimes were being committed against the planet and something had to be done."

"You sound like you're planning to defend me

yourself, Tom."

"No. I hired William Garner Chase for that."

Boxer's eyebrows went up. Chase was one of the best defense counsels in the world. He had a string of wins to his credit that would impress any jurist. Boxer could only wonder how much Stark had to pay for the man.

"I don't think I could afford him, Tom."

"*You* don't have to. He's working for bare minimum. Even I could pay the retainer. He is very active in environmental causes and he thinks what you've done is exemplary."

"I don't want to sound ungrateful, Tom, but does he know about maritime law?"

"If he doesn't, I'm sure he's getting a fast primer on it," Stark said.

"Does he know about UCMJ . . . the Uniform Code of Military Justice? You know, courts-martial are a lot different from civilian courts. Does he know?"

"Again, Jack, I'd have to say that if he doesn't, he's learning fast. I know UCMJ's tricky and a lot different from other codes. But . . . ?"

"Tom, I don't want to sound ungrateful but I think I want to handle my own defense."

"Jack, you're not a lawyer and this is a general court. You might know all of the procedures but a good maritime lawyer would tear you to ribbons."

"The second this starts, I'll make a motion to the president of the court about defending myself. There are provisions in UCMJ for it."

"I know there are . . . but . . . Jack, what about this? What about Chase as a legal advisor? He could sit at the table with you and you could ask his advice if you needed it."

He thought for a long moment before answering. Boxer had a great knowledge of naval law and had defended more than fifty special courts-martial in thirty years . . . where he faced only other non-lawyers. Though he managed to win well over forty of them, this was, after all, a General Court-Martial. His prosecution would be made up of a team of Naval officers who were lawyers as well as career officers. Yes, he thought, perhaps there was something in what Stark was saying. Perhaps there was a chance that William Garner Chase could be of some assistance in all of this. If nothing else, it was not throwing the offer of help back into his best friend's face.

"Okay, Tom. Perhaps you're right. I think it would be a good idea to have him there."

"Glad to hear you're thinking right," answered the former chief of naval operations. "Now we can start to get somewhere."

The Royal Dutch Shell Rig *Samar* was in just over a thousand feet of water on the edge of the Java trench. She was in a particularly precarious position because she sat like a house in the Los Angeles hills . . . one that stood out over the deep canyons on stilts. *Samar* was in about the same fix. She had the most dangerous position for a good reason; that position yielded the most oil from the strange geography of the trench. It was for this reason that RDS put Andre Doucette and his most experienced crew on the rig.

Doucette had been working for more than twenty-four hours on a sticky valve problem in the heli-ox system when he finally managed to solve the problem and turn in.

He was asleep for just over an hour when voices on the intercom woke him up.

"What the fuck is that?"

"It's a slave . . . a mandible . . . like an RMS."

The second voice was that of Charles Hedron, Doucette's operations chief. Doucette reached for the handset.

"Hedron! This is Doucette. What's going on?"

"We got a situation here, Captain. We . . ."

There was a sudden lurching jump and all of the alarm bells on the deep rig, which were keyed to movement, started to ring. Red emergency collision warning lights blinked. All hell broke loose.

"Will someone tell me what's happening? Did something hit us?" Doucette screamed into the mike while he tried to pull his coveralls on with his free hand.

"We got grabbed, Chief. Looks like a steel hawser line was attached by an RDS launched from something deep in the trench. The line heads down that way and there is a lot of bubble action in that direction."

"Why that lurch and the alarms?"

"Whatever the hell snagged us is pulling the rig in the direction of the trench."

Doucette could feel a ball of fear tighten in his stomach. It matched the chill that raced down the middle of his back.

Into the trench. There was close to three miles of water out there and it went straight down. If the rig broke free, she would fall like a rock. Even if she didn't batter herself to pieces on the sides of the cliff while she fell, there was a good chance that their pressure hull units wound start collapsing as they hit four to five thousand.

The *Samar* would implode!

Doucette was instantly fully awake. The threat of death had that impact on most people.

"Have you called the sur—" Another lurch grabbed at the *Samar.*

"Yes, sir," his OPS officer answered.

"Are they trying the back water against this? Where's security?"

"Security was diverted to a distress signal several miles away . . . clearly a ruse. The surface is using the umbilicus and the lifelines to back water against the pull. The best shot we have is to get a mobile into the water and cut the line with a mandible. Agree?"

Doucette had to think for a second before answering. He had to take into account the speed with which the crew could get to the jettisonable escape lockers similar to the ones that the *Deep Six* had. He reasoned that if the attempt to cut the line failed the crew would have enough time to get to the escape lockers.

"Go for it, OPS."

"I'm already in the mobile."

Doucette grimaced. OPS had been so sure he would agree. He didn't like anyone knowing him *that* well. "Move out, then. I'll get the rest of the crew into the coffins."

"On the way."

There was another sickening lurch and the metal framing of the *Samar* screamed under the stress. Doucette stabbed at the mike switch. "Hear this. This is Doucette. This is an emergency. All personnel except the watch officer lay to the coffins. When you get in, dog the hatches and pressurize."

Another lurch pulled the *Samar* into a sickeningly precarious angle, hanging over the side of the cliff. Death lay below.

Outside, Hedron was maneuvering in the direction of the cable that had snagged the rig and now threatened to pull it over the side into the black abyss. He had extended the line cutter so that he could snag it and crush it in one movement. This dual action was proving harder than he expected only minutes earlier. The line was weaving in several directions as if the ship pulling it was maneuvering left and right against deep water currents.

Another sickening lurch pulled the *Samar* until it seemed to hang at a ninety degree angle over the side of the cliff. Hedron managed to snag it and snap it in two. The free end whipped back into the trench like a snapped bullwhip. Hedron was glad he wasn't on the other side of the pull.

"OPS to *Samar*. Line freed. Say again. Line freed. Do you copy? Over."

"Copy, OPS." It was Doucette's voice. And, it sounded several decibels too high. "We have some other problems here. Stay out there and give us some observation."

"Staying on station."

On the *Samar*, Doucette was trying to rebalance the rig without creating too much turmoil. She was literally hanging by a thread.

"Engineering. Get me seawater shifted from tanks A-sixteen to R-forty-four. Copy?"

A voice from the engineering area answered. In a matter of minutes, the seawater was shifted. It was a technique designed for just such an emergency. It shifted ballast as a surface ship might to trim itself. The *Samar* was trying to gain more purchase on the uncertain cliff ledge. "Now shift B-three to R-twenty-one. Copy?"

"Copy." Again, the same voice.

He was waiting for the confirmation of the shift when everything went insane.

There was a nauseating, skidding sound, punctuated by all of the Klaxons screaming and collision lights flashing.

Doucette thought of his dead wife and of the two children he was going to orphan on the surface.

"Away all escape lockers. Away all escape lockers."

He knew he would not have time to get to one himself. In another second, he would start to hear the scream of compressed air as the lockers fired themselves away from the slipping rig that was starting to gather speed as it fell.

The last of the lockers was gone for fifteen seconds and Doucette was sure that he was in the neighborhood of five thousand feet when the first of the pressure hulls started to collapse. At a mile and a half, the small pod that Doucette was in collapsed . . . imploded. In a split second, Doucette was crushed by billions of tons of seawater.

Close to a mile above and three miles away, a Merc commander watched his side scanning sonar array.

He nodded in satisfaction. "Breaking up. Good. Inform Tosenko we have been successful."

"Aye, aye, sir," a second in command said a few feet away.

"Oh, and see to it that none of those escape trunks makes it to the surface. And sink that mechanical that cut the line."

"Sir?"

The second in command did not question the efficiency of the act. He was concerned about the death of brave men who really did not, in his view, have to die.

The leader did not like his orders questioned.

"Do as you are told."

"Aye, aye, sir."

After a pause, the man in charge spoke again.

"You know the proverb, don't you?"

"What proverb is that, sir?"

"It comes from the English pirate named William Kidd?"

"I am sorry. I don't know that one, sir."

There was a pause while the commander sensed the dramatic.

"The pirate always worked at avoiding detection by killing all of the people on the ships he plundered. He assumed that it would keep him from the rope if he was somehow captured. In fact, it didn't. They did capture and eventually hang him."

"And the proverb, sir?"

"Oh yes, the proverb. Dead men tell no tales."

Chapter Six

The cell was getting smaller and smaller, Boxer thought. Actually, it wasn't. It was that it had been filled with more and more things. Many of them were law books. He had not regretted taking the immense responsibility of his own defense until he found that his tiny living space was further diminished by all of the law books and files that were coin of the realm for lawyers.

William Garner Chase had been in to see Boxer a number of times. He possessed a greater insight into maritime law than Boxer ever imagined the man might have had, being a chair bound lawyer.

"Prisoner Boxer."

It was the Lance Corporal, who was not allowed to use rank when speaking to prisoners.

"Yes?"

"You have a visitor."

"Who is it this time?"

"Someone connected to your defense. That's all I know, sir."

They headed out of the cell block through the now

familiar path that led to the visitor's area. When Boxer turned into the small phone booth area, another familiar and utterly unexpected face met him.

"Borodine!"

"Good day, Admiral. I trust they are treating you well?"

"As well as the KGB if I were in the Lubianka."

He knew that the response would tell Borodine everything he wanted to communicate.

"Of course . . . understood, Admiral. However, you must remember that in the CIS unlike the old USSR, there is no KGB and there is no more Lubianka."

"Russia won't seem like Russia any more, Borodine. Are they going to tear it down for a parking lot?"

"Something like that. A Mac-something or other, too. One of those food places that dispenses cholesterol."

Boxer laughed for the first time in a week.

They managed to mollify the possible eavesdroppers with some small talk before they got down to business. They spoke as cryptically and elliptically as possible to forestall immediate recognition of what they were saying. They had no way of telling if it would work.

"The report that I wrote about our recent mission?" Borodine began.

"Yes? How did it sit with your superiors?"

"That has provided a problem, Admiral. It seems that the report ended up on the desk of a consular official here in the United States . . . in New York, specifically."

"How is it that it didn't end up in the Kremlin?"

"It started there and was . . . diverted. I am not

sure yet how that happened. These days all of the old patterns are changing. The only loyalty is capital . . . frightening, isn't it?"

Boxer knew instantly what the man was talking about. What had happened was that high-level officials in the Kremlin had been bought with a great deal of money. And, the coin of the realm was not rubles. It was American dollars or Swiss francs or something equally solvent.

"Is there a line on this official?"

"If you mean by that, is there a chance of getting information from him, I would say there is a very good chance." Borodine smiled. "The man is in New York and a representative of Russia . . . that is Great Russia, former Comrade Yeltsin's Great Russia. He thinks he has a post in the new consulate. But, who is to know these days? The man's name is Tosenko . . . Arkady Tosenko. And he is, you might say . . . reachable."

Boxer construed that this also meant for a fee, and he was sure that Stark would pay the fee for him.

"Is he sufficiently reachable that he could be brought to my trial and made to testify under oath about the materials he intercepted?"

Boxer watched as Borodine scratched his head for a second. It was a lot to ask and both men knew it.

"For this it would require, I think, that we dig up a great many family skeletons for former Comrade Tosenko. There is a chance that this can be done. Yes. I will do my best."

Borodine paused and thought for a moment. It was more a pause to confirm the way he was going to handle the next bit of information than anything else. He had always been a bit awkward at passing on personal messages . . . especially of this type. For his own strange reasons, Borodine was more comfortable telling a man his family had just died than a woman was sending her regards. As he had grown well into middle age, he had started to see this as a weak point in his own personality. Though, he had never managed to do much about it.

"I have greetings from a certain comrade or former comrade doctor in your acquaintance."

Boxer could not resist a smile though his memories of Ilia Ioff were mixed. She was a considerable woman but in the final analysis, perhaps too professional and aloof for him . . . not nearly dependent enough. And despite the fact that she was more than a little attracted to him and he to her, anything substantial was out of the question because of a clash of near generations.

"She, as I say, is concerned about your health and welfare."

"But not with enough concern to come here and see me personally."

Borodine spread his hands in a gesture that could only mean a lack of understanding. Either he didn't understand Boxer's remark or Ioff's comments or human relationships in general.

Boxer waved the gesture aside. "Just tell her, my friend, if she wants to inquire about my health, I suggest she come here in person and see me. By the way, is she still involved with my old friend the secretary of the Navy?"

Borodine blinked. "I had no idea she ever was so involved. My opinion of the good doctor just went up . . . a great deal. And I will pass on the information."

The two men hung up their respective phones and Boxer faced the long walk back to the tiny cell and the law books that had become his companions. A dark cape of utter depression descended on him before he could even see it coming.

In the immense Langley complex, photoanalysis of SAT map materials showed plumes of smoke in the Java strike as well as swirls of oil in the water spreading more than a thousand miles from the Java trench. Harry Olsen looked forlornly at the mosaic. Cosgrove stood a few feet away. Olsen looked up from the photos that had been shot from more than twenty-four thousand miles in space.

"What's the vintage on this?" The age of intelligence photos had for some time been likened to the vintage of old wines within the confines of Langley. However, with typical intelligence community perverseness, the older the vintage of photo the poorer the taste of the wine. Stuff hot from the telemetry printer was considered best as it was the closest to real time imagery.

Cosgrove checked his watches . . . he wore one on each wrist. The right was set to Greenwich Mean Time; the one on the left was local. It was the same kind of arrangements that diplomatic couriers used to use.

"Ninety-four minutes from image completion, sir. That would make the image itself three and a half hours old. I've ordered another scan on the next pass. We will have that this afternoon local time."

"Very well. Do we have anything from our field people on site?"

"One report from a man we have with a rig owned by British petroleum. He says the rig slipped off the edge of the trench."

"How the hell could that happen?" Olsen asked.

Cosgrove looked through a neatly arranged stack of papers he had attached to his clipboard. It took him only a second or two to extract the one he wanted. "It seems that the position of the *Samar* was the most precarious of any of the deep drilling habitats in the area. He said he thought there might have been a gravity slide . . . so slight it went unnoticed on the surface but it took the *Samar* off the edge."

Olsen cocked his head to the side. "What do you think the chances of that are?"

"Very slim, sir," Cosgrove said. "I called the national recording centers in New York and in Denver. They had nothing. If a gnat farts they can record it."

"So, the machine was done in like the rest?"

"It would seem so, sir."

"And has this hit the press?" Olsen asked.

"Not the print media. That will take another few hours."

"The networks, then?"

"The three majors caught it about fifteen minutes ago. I expect that the independents will be along any time with bulletins."

"Has there been a chance to see if there has been a reaction on world oil markets?"

"I have a team working on that, sir. I expect that they'll have an analysis on this by perhaps 3:30 P.M. this afternoon. We won't have the Nikkei as it won't have opened yet. But we will have a pretty good picture from the Zurich, London, and New York."

"Good work, Em. Keep on this."

"Yes, sir."

Olsen stabbed at the button on his intercom. "Get me the White House Chief of Staff." He looked back to Cosgrove. "I'm going to have to get in to see the Old Man before I wanted to. If this stuff takes the price of oil any higher he's out of a job in November. We are, too."

Von Stempler was reading abstracts of the press notices Boxer had managed to get. They would have been infuriating if Von Stempler was a man to get angry but Eric Von was not a man to lose his temper. In the vernacular he preferred to get even rather than mad. He had every faith in the world that Boxer was going to be convicted. He spent enough money on the members of the court-martial who could be bought to assure that, but he was concerned that the unforeseen would occur. There was always the chance of a double cross by someone already paid. There was a possibility that a member of the court or some other person in the legal proceeding would come clean and blow the story to the media. If there was anyone in the world capable of destroying more of Eric Von's holdings, it was Boxer and no one else.

The solution was simple. Boxer had to be taken out

before he came to trial. Arrange for a neat suicide in his cell. Arrange for a fall from the cell block. Eric Von's spies had already informed him that Boxer's cell was on the third tier. But, he didn't even have to worry about that. All he had to do was hire the right man for the job and make sure that it was done. Tactics could be left to the professional.

"I don't want to know your name," Von Stempler said quietly to the well-dressed man in his thirties who sat across the desk. The man seemed composed beyond his years. He had come highly recommended. He was expensive . . . but hopefully worth it.

"There are not more than a few people in the world who do," the man said with a smile.

Von Stempler met the young man's smile with his own. "The target is a man named Boxer . . . Admiral Boxer. He has recently cost me a great deal of money."

The young man raised a hand. "As you did not want to know my name, I do not need to know the list of offenses that the target, this Admiral Boxer, has committed. The fact that he is a target suffices. Where is he?"

"He is currently in the United States in a Navy prison in Norfolk."

The man's eyebrows went up a fraction of an inch.

"That will require some additional preparation."

"Are you saying that you can't do the job?" Von Stempler asked, surprised at the remark.

"Not at all. There is a greater than average risk factor . . . but the job can be carried out. Is there a need for this to look like an . . . 'unfortunate accident'?"

"It would perhaps be best that way," Von Stempler intoned.

"That, unfortunately, will also cost a bit more than the normal rate. There are things to be considered . . . covering the trail and such. I'm sure you understand?"

"Of course." Eric Von managed an engaging smile. He was already planning the demise of the hit man when the job was done.

Secretary of the Navy Smith and Navy Chief of Staff Hale met in the anteroom to the Oval Office. Both men instantly felt awkward. Neither had known that the President had summoned them both and that was apparently what the President had wanted them to know . . . or not know.

The old man was strange that way, Smith thought.

"What's he up to? Do you know?" he asked Hale. The Navy chief of staff simply stared at him and spread his hands in a helpless gesture.

They were ushered in and were seated across from the President on one of two sofas that straddled an ornate coffee table.

"Can I offer either of you coffee? Or, perhaps something stronger?"

Both men looked to one another. Neither had seen the President offer anything more than coffee before the sun was down. Something had to be seriously wrong.

"Coffee will be fine, Mister President," Smith, the

senior of the two responded.

"Take a look at that pile of mail, gentlemen." The President pointed to a sack of mail that had been opened and emptied in the corner.

It was clear that the President, who was always fond of object lessons, was about to start one.

They both looked and then looked back to "The Man."

"That pile represents a small part of the daily arrival that comes into this building. Specifically, it represents only letters supporting Admiral Jack Boxer and the actions he carried out in that area of the North Pacific that is fast getting to be called the hot zone."

Both men nodded solemnly.

"So, when there are this many letters . . . I believe the count is fifteen or twenty thousand right now . . . I have to be concerned. Just what are the chances of his being convicted on this charge of piracy?"

Smith spoke first. "The crime is one of the most serious among all maritime crimes. Generally, piracy has meant a death penalty. Boxer stole an American submarine when it was in commissioned status and took it to carry out an adventurous mission in the North Pacific. It's all pretty straight forward, Mister President."

"I don't know how straight forward it could be if I am getting this many letters from those people and groups that sympathize with him. He's become the messiah of the environmentalist movement. If the court-martial board deals *too* harshly with him and his crew, the Navy will get a great deal of bad ink about this."

Both men knew that the President was not talking about the bad press the Navy would be getting as much as the bad press that *he* would be getting . . . especially in an election year.

"Mister President? I really have to say this," Hale interrupted. "I personally think that Boxer's actions have to be applauded more than condemned. He managed to uncover a nuclear waste dump that could have grown with outcomes for the planet that he could not even begin to consider. The only way he could manage to pull it off was to hijack the SSN-S1 and take it out there. I am sure that he was certain that a court-martial was in the offing if he were caught. I'm sorry, Mister President. I am forced to disagree with the secretary. Boxer is to be applauded."

"Well," the President looked to Smith and then to Hale. "I think I have to agree myself. You'll remember Mister Secretary, I was once in the Navy and I know the meaning of military discipline and the seriousness of piracy. But there *are* mitigating circumstances for everything."

The President shifted uneasily in his chair. "I want to meet this man Boxer quietly and as soon as can reasonably be arranged. Do either of you see any difficulty in that?"

Both men looked at one another. What the President was asking was highly irregular. But, after all, he was the *President* and what he asked would be done. It was Smith who answered as it was his place to.

"Mister President, I am certain that we will be able to set up a totally confidential meeting. And, I am sure that you have your reasons for wanting to meet the man. But, I can only wonder at your motives."

The President stared at him. He was not used to having his motives questioned in any event. It was something that simply did not happen in the Oval Office.

"You let me worry about the motives," the President said, with a strident quality that was just on the far edge of anger. "I want to see him. And, what I require is secrecy. I'm certain that you can handle that."

"Admiral Boxer?"

The hackles rose on Boxer's neck as he heard the name no guard had spoken from the time he arrived in the brig.

He was seated on the small desk chair with his back to the door and was halfway through a chapter of a maritime law tome.

"Yes?" he answered as he rose to a low crouch.

"You have a visitor," the voice said calmly.

Boxer was sure that there was no visitor and he doubted the intentions this marine who he could barely see in the small hand mirror that hung from his bunk. He was not the usual one, and he had called Boxer by rank. All prisoners in the brig were ranked as seaman recruit and so there were no titles. When and if officers were incarcerated, they were not treated with more deference than any other prisoner. Something was *terribly* wrong.

He got to his feet and turned to look at the man. He was in the same impeccable uniform that the other guard wore and his manner was as soldierly. But Boxer's antennae were up and there was something afoot.

"Seems an odd time for visitors. I usually get them in the morning." A glance to the small travel clock on his tray desk told him that it was after 6 P.M. in the evening.

No! This was not about visitors.

"There is someone, sir."

Boxer managed a smile. "Well, if there is . . . there is. Do you know *who?*"

"No, sir. I was ordered to bring you. That's all I know."

A lie. An out and out lie. And, Boxer knew it. He tried to betray nothing as he moved to the cell door.

The young man he was looking at was in peak physical shape and less than half Boxer's age. He would be quick and strong and skilled. Boxer had a single advantage if experience was ruled out. He *knew.* Something was about to happen and he was not sure what it was.

He was not going to have long to wait.

He left through the cell door and turned left. He was a few feet down the walkway of the third tier when Boxer saw the move. It came in the most unlikely of ways. He saw the dozen or so cells in front of them and a number of the prisoners had perched mirrors up so that they could see what was going on at the other end of the bay. It was in one of the mirrors that Boxer caught a flicker of movement.

The guard was slipping something from his blouse pocket.

Boxer recognized what it was. A hypodermic needle!

He could not see the hand that held the needle raise to strike but he could sense that it was happening.

He waited only another split second.

He spun. His timing had been right. The man's right hand was at the top of its arc. He was about to plunge the needle into Boxer.

Boxer drove forward with a fist to the midsection of the man, but he danced away holding the hypo as if it were a switchblade knife and he was in a knife fight.

Boxer moved in a step. He was smaller than his attacker by an inch or two and he yielded thirty or more years to the man. His reflexes were no match for this would-be assassin. The assassin feinted high and drove the hypo up in an arc from below, hoping to bury it and what had to be its deadly content in Boxer's gut. Boxer held his cupped hands down to meet the approaching arm. He managed to grasp the assailant's hypo as it came upward while avoiding the deadly venom it contained.

He snapped the hand to the right and swung it at a crazy angle until the hypodermic dropped from the man's hands. It clattered to the grate and rolled off the side, falling down three tiers to the bottom cell block.

He wasn't out of the woods, yet. The assassin dipped a shoulder and charged, looking to tumble him to the grating and then either roll him or throw him off the catwalk.

Boxer sidestepped and, with greater speed than his attacker thought possible in a man his age, dove to the back of the attacker.

He managed to snake a hand around the man's throat and pull while he counterbalanced with a hand behind the neck. He applied pressure both ways. It was not going to take long before he broke the man's neck.

"Who? Who paid you?"

The man said nothing.

Boxer increased the strength of his grip. He could hear the man start to gurgle. The attacker was also trying to get his head to the side so that he could use the muscles of the neck to allow the larynx to flex and to get some air.

Boxer squeezed harder.

"Who? Who paid you?"

There was no answer. The man simply tried to move his head from side to side against the immense pressure that Boxer was applying.

Then, Boxer heard it happen.

A crunch! It was not the man's neck. Boxer would have squeezed much harder for that.

He had bitten into something and Boxer was fairly sure what it was. He let go of the man's neck and quickly rolled him over. The man was already starting to spasm.

Shellfish toxin . . . he was fairly sure. There was little else that was quite so fast and sure.

"Shit!" he snarled aloud. Now there would be no way of knowing.

"Freeze!"

He heard a voice behind him. A marine had heard the shouting of the prisoners and came running. The man was standing with a .45 in his hand, and the weapon was little more than three inches from Boxer's head. Boxer froze.

"This was an assassination attempt. This man was not part of the staff," Boxer explained evenly.

The marine pulled a whistle from his uniform shirt and blew it frantically. The echoes rebounded through the cell block.

Rattled and ashen, Boxer was led back in the direction of his cell.

"Tried to *kill* him? Who the fuck tried to kill him?" The President shrieked.

William Smith stood at something resembling attention at the desk of the Commander in Chief's Oval Office and answered with the best skill he could muster.

"We have no idea. The man entered the building with the correct credentials . . . excellent forgeries. He managed to get to the cell and knew exactly where it was. He was a professional, there's no mistaking that."

"I want all of the securities gone over. I want that man protected."

Smith did not bother to tell the President that the procedures had already been gone over five times and there was a good chance that they would be gone over yet another five before the day was over. The old man was simply pissed.

"Sir, we can move the admiral to another location . . . a more secret one and only let him out for the trial. We have done such things before."

"Do what you have to. I want him safe. And I want to speak to him. I'll get the NSA to handle it. I want you folks out of this part of the loop."

The secretary cringed but took the rebuke. "We'll move him, sir."

The President's mood brightened. "Old guy fought like a son of a bitch, they say."

"Yes, sir. The report indicated that the assassin swallowed a substance and would not have done that if he thought there was a chance of escape."

The President grinned for the barest split second.

"Yes," he intoned. "I do want to meet this man."

Chapter Seven

It was raining lightly in the prison yard when Boxer, alone as usual, was allowed his daily exercise. His goal was to find how damaged his body had *really* been in the exchange with the assassin. This could not be done through the standard set of exercises that the Service had prescribed for years. It needed special and specific diagnosis. The Navy surgeon who had examined him after the attack had told him that minor contusions and a few muscle pulls were all that had happened. Boxer had to know for himself.

He cleared his mind and set his feet a comfortable distance apart and crouched slightly flexing his quads in the opening stance of the T'ai Chi "Riding Horse" exercise. Each of the patterned and choreographed movements brought the mind and body into perfect harmony. All of the muscle groups were brought into play. The set of exercises was nearly three thousand years old and had been keeping the Chinese in condition for most of that time.

He determined that the low back and the left deltoids were the most damaged areas. But, it had not taken the

T'ai Chi to apprise that. Both of those areas had made their irritability clear to him when he had awoken on the steel springed brig bunk at 5:00 A.M.

He looked at the gray Virginia sky and saw that a few breaks in the clouds had promised better weather for the afternoon. There would also be heat . . . the Virginia heat that he remembered so many times when he had put a submarine into Norfolk in the thirty odd years he had spent in the Navy. The pain in his back and in his left arm started to intensify as a small wave of depression washed across him. How many subs had he brought into the yard? How many times had he flown the broom of the clean sweep? And, this was the way his country had thanked him?

Son of a bitch! No! He would not have it this way! He would not cave in to depression and rage at the Navy. He loved the Navy as he always had loved her. What he hated was the greed and ambition that men had brought to her. And he had to admit it . . . it was the lesser men most of the time.

It was the deskbound book men and armchair admirals who had succumbed to the greed for rank and privilege. They were the ones who had avoided the action that Boxer had thrived on for so many years. *They* were the *enemy* . . . not the Navy.

He let his mind flow back into the river that was the Tao and he moved with the classic form of the *Hai-Dachi* . . . the mimed mounted combat that had been part of what the Mongolians had brought with them to China when they came as conquerors.

He had started the third of what would be five repetitions of the exercise when he saw the two men come into the yard.

They were government . . . that was certain. Their business suits with jackets two sizes larger than trousers were what gave that away. The extra room was for body armor and a sizeable sidearm. They were young and athletic and, Boxer thought, they could kill him in a few seconds if they were of a mind to. He had no place to run and nothing with which to fight.

He did not stop the exercise. It would come to a natural conclusion in less than thirty seconds anyway. The men kept their distance seemingly out of respect and Boxer thought that boded well. At least the chances were good that he would get to finish the exercise alive.

He had managed to complete the repetition and had started a series of rhythmic breathing exercises when they decided to approach. When they got to arm's distance, Boxer thought he recognized one of the men, though he could not place him. As things turned out, he was right. He had seen the tall, slender man a number of times in the past when he had been at briefings at NSA headquarters.

The tall man whose name Boxer did not remember spoke first. And, he actually smiled.

"Admiral Boxer? We know this is the only time you get outside your cell during the day. But, we need to talk with you."

Boxer smiled. "How can I resist a smooth line like that?"

This time both men laughed. They ushered Boxer through a door in another part of the yard, and through as series of halls that he had not yet seen. They seemed to walk for fifteen minutes and make half a dozen turns. Boxer was not entirely sure that he could backtrack the steps they had taken.

They turned into a final hall and the decor brightened a great deal. They had moved into an administrative area and one that was used to getting visitors. They headed in the direction of a door where two armed guards waited. When they got to the door, the man whom Boxer recognized by sight turned to him.

"There is an individual in the room waiting for you. You will be meeting with this individual for a time and when you come back from the room there will be no record of the meeting. The meeting will simply have not happened. Is that clear?"

Boxer nodded.

"I'm sorry, Admiral. I have to get a verbal answer from you. Will you agree that when this encounter is over . . . all parties will agree that it never happened?"

Boxer shrugged. "As much as I hate to mention it, given my present circumstances, what is in it for me if I agree?"

The man smiled. "I understand. But, I can't tell you, Admiral. The one you are meeting on the other side of the door is in a better position than I to tell you about the things that you might gain by such an agreement. But, of course, you have to agree before you can get in in the first place."

"Catch-22, then?" Boxer asked.

"Something like that," the man said.

Boxer paused, weighing the options. If he did not agree to be silent about the meeting then he would not get to the meeting in the first place. He had to agree, if for no other reason than to sate his incredible curiosity.

"Very well. I agree."

The guard, who Boxer thought had to be from the

National Security Agency, smiled and turned opening the door.

Boxer entered and, realizing he was in an L-shaped room, turned to his left.

He found himself facing the President of the United States.

"Admiral Boxer, I presume?"

"Ah . . . yes . . . M-Mister President."

The President laughed. "Well, it's good to see that even the daring Admiral Jack Boxer can be taken by surprise once in a while."

"It's not every day that he gets to meet the Commander in Chief, sir," Boxer said tentatively. He had no idea in the world what the meeting could be about.

The room was a well-appointed office, and the only convenience it seemed to be missing was a window. The President gestured in the direction of a chair that sat opposite a small desk.

Boxer took the seat offered and the President moved behind the desk.

It was only after both men were seated that the President spoke.

"Admiral . . . I feel I know you. And, as a politician, may I call you Jack?"

"Of course, Mister President."

"Well, Jack, they tell me that this room is utterly free of electronic devices and the possibility of such devices. I don't know a great deal about such things but I do know when my electronics people tell me we're not bugged, I believe them. So, we can speak freely here, Jack.

"I'm sure you know about the amount of support you have gotten from the press and the ranks of the environmentalists in this hot zone matter?"

"Not really, sir. I have heard a thing or two from some of my visitors."

The President frowned. "False modesty does not become you Admiral Boxer. It sort of sits there like three-day-old fish. Half the country is on your side about this thing and I have a hunch you not only know it, but you are preparing a defense based on it."

"Yes, sir."

"I am also told that despite the fact that Admiral Stark has gotten William Garner Chase for your defense counsel, you insist on defending yourself? Is that correct, also?"

"It is . . . Mister President."

"Is there a reason for that, Jack?"

"I thought that given the intricacies of the Uniform Code of Military Justice, Mister President, Mister Garner would not have time to get familiar with the differences between it and civilian law. He never has tried a court-martial case, sir."

"I know that he hasn't. But, he has a staff that could gather more than you know in a third of the time from now to your trial. They are professionals, Jack. Well, you have made a decision you will have to live with. Be that as it may. We have to talk about some other things, Jack. Basically, I have to ask you some questions."

"Yes, sir . . . Mister President." Some of the shock had worn off but Boxer was still unable to grasp why the President had a need to talk with him.

The President paused before looking back to Boxer across the desk.

"The charge that they have leveled against you is piracy as I am sure you know."

"They made that rather clear, Mister President."

98

The President smiled at Boxer's attitude and his wry sense of humor.

"Well, I went over the charges and they *are* considerable. There seems to be little sense in your pleading not guilty to such charges given where Admiral Kirkson found you and the SSN-S1."

Boxer shook his head and smiled again. "No, Mister President, there is little chance in pleading that we were not where we were found."

"Well, now we've established that you were where you were, and you were there because you wanted to be. I guess the next order of business is the real reason you were there and the desperate need that took you there, even at the cost of stealing a US submarine to do so."

"Are you asking me why I did it? Is that the reason for this, Mister President? If that's the case, you can read the transcript of the court-martial. Or, you can read my memoirs. Why would you have to know that, Mister President?"

"You have a Navy Cross, Jack. I'm sure you have read the histories of men who have been awarded the Congressional Medal of Honor. One of the things that they have in common is that had they not been awarded the CMH, there is a good chance that they would have been court-martialed for the actions they carried out."

"Is that your concern here, Mister President?"

"No . . . not quite. I don't think anyone who had been nominated for a CMH had ever stolen a Navy vessel to carry out the mission.

"No, Jack. My concern is personal curiosity. I have to satisfy something in my own head. Why did you do it? Was the crew a volunteer operation?"

"Of course. And, Mister President, every one of

them knew that there was a chance that they would end up at the end of a rope. What they did . . . what I did was something that had to be done?"

"Why?"

"Because, they were demolishing the oceans with the dumping. The fishing was going and there was a chance it would be gone in a matter of a few years. Not to mention, there was a chance that the fish being caught and marketed were already hot."

"So the concern was environmental, then?" the President asked tentatively.

"No. . . . Yes. More than that. There's something else, Mister President. You know how the world is run. It's not a matter of nationalities as much as profit and loss statements. The world is run by folks who have little concern for more than the next quarterly profit statement. The power groups have been around for decades . . . the Bilderbergers . . . the Trilateral Commission . . . the International Consortium. Between them they control all of it and it's high time it gets returned to the people. I know this sounds like an idealistic monologue, but I mean it. The people are having the planet poisoned under them and they don't even know it. Soon, they will be handed the bill to clean up the mess . . . if they can clean it up. The ones who made a fortune poisoning it will walk away scot-free. I had to close up the hot zone. A lot of people were killed when I tried to publicize it, and they deserved to have the job done. End of speech . . . Mister President."

It was as if Boxer had not ventilated his feelings in years. He felt like fifty pounds of lead had been lifted from his back. The President, on the other hand, looked somber.

"I get the distinct impression that you would have a short, but illustrious, career in politics, Admiral." Finally, Boxer smiled.

"No thanks, Mister President. I leave that to you. I'm just a sailor. Though . . . I might not be for long."

The President cleared his throat and looked into Boxer's eyes.

"Jack, I admire you. I admire what you have done. The organizations you mentioned are the power structures of the world. There is a chance that your method was the only one that could have gotten results. I applaud the fact that you did what you did for your dead friends. Privately, I applaud you. You must understand something, though."

Boxer knew what was coming or at least he thought he did.

"What's that, sir?"

"There is no way that I can intercede in your trial or the result. Things must run their course. What I can do is put the most understanding men in the court-martial proceedings that I can find."

"No one could ask anything more than that, Mister President."

The President came around the desk and shook Boxer's hand. "Good luck, Jack, and God bless you."

Boxer threw the President a salute, and the Commander in Chief returned it, then turned to leave through the door at the opposite end of the room. He stopped and turned back as he opened the door.

"Another thing. Please remember this conversation never took place."

"What conversation?" Boxer smiled.

The President nodded and closed the door. Boxer did

not notice the trip back through the exercise yard and the climb up to the third tier. What surprised him when he got to his cell was that everything has been moved out. All that was left in the cell were his personal effects. All of the law books, the typewriter and everything else that had made the cell feel so small had been taken out.

Boxer turned to the guard. "What happened to it all?"

"You are being moved, Admiral." Suddenly, his rank was being used also. What was happening?

Also, he found himself cringing at the sound of his rank spoken by a Marine guard. He knew there was little reason to let it rattle him now. But, it still did.

"Where am I being moved and why now?"

Boxer found himself suspicious of everything. The marine looked impassive. "Orders to put you in trustee status, Admiral. Some of the status of rank has been returned. Orders, sir."

The new cell was something more of a BOQ room than a cell. There was an outside window and, except for the fact that the door was locked most of the time and there were bars on the window, Boxer might have thought that he was in a moderately priced civilian motel.

He had the privilege of a bathroom and a shower, though there were surveillance cameras on the walls . . . even in the bathroom. It didn't matter. It allowed Boxer to have a hot shower when he wanted rather than being marched to the gang showers where cold water was the daily bill of fare.

Boxer wondered if the non-meeting with the Commander in Chief had this effect on his status. Or, was it the pressure the Navy was getting from the press? When he was five minutes into a hot needle point shower, he

102

didn't care if the Pope had intervened. He was starting to feel more like a naval officer again and less like a prisoner.

It was a day or two of his changed circumstances that started to make Boxer worry about the progress of his case. He realized that the President and Stark had both been right about his use of William Garner Chase in his defense. He decided to speak to the man and have him take a greater role in the case. His conversation or "non-conversation" with the President had reached him. He could not afford to be so arrogant as to expect an acquittal at his own hands.

It was three days after he had been moved that Ilia visited him.

He looked across the glass at her and was overcome with the urge to smash the glass and just hold her . . . well more than hold her. He had been in the brig for some time now and his physical pressure cooker could only be kept at bay by so much T'ai Chi. After a while it would blow its top.

"How are you?" she whispered into the handset, her voice was honey and her body was luscious. She wore a white, silk summer dress and he could see her nipples pressing through her bra and outlining themselves in the filmy dress.

Boxer gulped before he answered.

"As well as can be expected."

"I have a great deal of news. Some of it is going to have to do with the trial and then . . . there are *other* things."

He did not like the sound of the *other* things, and he almost asked her to speak about them right away. But, Ilia was very much her own woman and she would come to things when she was ready and not a moment before.

"Am I still in the news? It's important. If I managed to slip into the background, then I'm sunk."

"Your friend . . . Carol Benson . . . has managed to create a one-woman media blitz on your account. She had kept you on every front page that she could manage to. There are some papers and TV programs that have dropped you as a topic of conversation as, she informs me, some news directors see you and the whole hot zone incident as a piece of old news now."

Boxer smiled broadly. He would have to find a special way to thank Carol, he thought.

Ilia almost intercepted the thought. Her tone chilled, or at least Boxer thought it did.

"This next is something it is hard to talk about and it is something I cannot do anything about. I almost don't want to mention it."

"Spit it out, darlin'. We gotta have it all."

"It seems Admiral Borodine has been recalled to the CIS, specifically to Russia . . . Moscow for what the government is calling 'consultations.' I don't like the sound of it. He had been given very little warning in this. He managed to tell me before he went that he thought it had something to do with the report on the hot zone and the specific Russian gentleman he was trying to recruit to be a hostile witness for the defense.

"He managed to tell me before he left that he had also found that the Russian you had been after . . . had *died* . . . he thought."

"Died? Was he sure?"

"He thought so."

"How *seriously* did he think?"

"It is hard to say. You know Borodine. He was not

prone to speak with mathematical precision about anything except the management of a submarine."

"So the report on the hot zone operation is lost perhaps somewhere in the secretary of the Navy's office. And the man Borodine had been after has died and that prevents the report from getting to Russia?"

"It would seem that way, Jack."

"Was there any indication of how he was killed?"

"The method?"

"Yes."

"He said the man was seemingly poisoned . . . it was only a preliminary report."

"I would bet a month's pay that they found shellfish toxin in the toxicology screen."

Ilia's eyes went wide for a fraction of a second.

"How could you have known that?"

"It was a good guess."

"It makes you sad, Jack. It would have to. You were counting on Borodine helping you and finding this man?"

"For sure."

"Is there anything else I can do?"

Again, he could see her nipples standing at semi-attention and pressing through the white summer dress.

"Nothing you can do through the glass and over the phone . . . not unless this is one of those 900 lines."

"I am not sure what a 900 line is, but I think I understand the rest of what you said. I am flattered."

"I want you to be flattered, Ilia. I am tempted to ask what happened with Smith. But, I don't know if I should."

"I think you already have, Jack."

There was an awkward silence for a long moment before Ilia spoke.

"I think it was you who were the one who said that all good things must come to an end?"

"I wasn't the first but I was one of the many to say it . . . yes."

"Well, it just didn't work . . . it didn't take. The real thing is very hard to find, Jack."

"I know, Ilia. I know. . . ."

Another silence ebbed between them. It was Boxer who broke it.

"And, what's in store for you now? When we started to the hot zone you had the USSR, and now it's the CIS. There's a whole new bureaucracy back there."

"I am going to go back, Jack. There are people back there who need me . . . especially now."

Boxer could feel a part of his heart tear from him. He tried not to show it.

"Will you stay for the court-martial?"

"I was there. I was only not charged because I am a CIS foreign national as was Borodine. Of course, I will be there. No matter what the outcome, I will be there for it and leave right after."

"Thank you, Ilia. And, I am so very sorry about Smith. Sorry for you . . . not for him."

"There is no room in my heart for any sorrow at all, Jack. Perhaps there will be, later. But now, there is none. Your words are kind. Goodbye. *Do Svidanya, Tovarich.*"

And, she was gone.

Depression slipped over Boxer like a dark cape. There was no chance in the world that he could ever get acquitted now. What he had told the President was true, the forces were too large. They moved and shaped the financial structure of the world and they were the ones who had stolen the Russian sailors' bodies, murdered Kate, misdirected reports and, ultimately, silenced the key figure who Borodine was after.

He could see them chewing him up and spitting him out at the court-martial. One did not go through a career in the service and not make enemies who would wait for the day when you were most vulnerable.

For Jack Boxer that day was only a week and a half away. It would be the day of the convening of his General Court-Martial.

Chapter Eight

"Attention!"

The spectators along with the trial and defense counsels were on their feet as the members of the court-martial board moved into the table that had been reserved for them. The trial was being held in a large airplane hangar at the far end of the Norfolk Naval Base. There were literally thousands of people who had wanted to attend the trial but the Navy insured that the numbers were kept to a reasonable size. The gallery of spectators was limited to three hundred and these seats had been raffled off in a lottery. More than two thousand people had applied.

Boxer came to his feet as the four members of the board strode into the room. He wore every decoration he had ever been awarded, including the foreign ones. They added up to five rows of ribbons . . . a spectacular amount of "fruit salad" for any one career officer.

William Garner Chase stood next to him and watched as the four remaining members of the board pulled out their chairs.

Originally, there had been seven members of the

board. There were seven on all Special and General Courts-Martial across the services. The Trial Counsel, which was what the service called the prosecution, and the defense counsel each had a "free" challenge and then a number of challenges that needed to be substantiated. There was a tactic to all of this as Chase explained to Boxer.

Unlike the civilian jury, the number of members on a court-martial board was flexible. The minimum needed was three members. Also, there was no need for a unanimous count for a guilty vote. What was needed was a simple majority. So, it behooved the prosecution to convince as small a majority as possible. The defense angled the board to the point where he had to convince the fewest members of the court to get an acquittal. In this case, Chase and the Trial Counsel, Rear Admiral Thomas Gaines, had managed to get to four which favored Boxer. Gaines had to convince three of the board members and Chase had to persuade only two of Boxer's innocence.

"Be seated," the admiral, who was the remaining flag officer on the board, said.

What followed was the reading of the charges and specifications lodged against Boxer. The trial of the others, Sarkis and the crewmen, had been severed from his own. He and Chase had hoped that the severance would make the trial of the subordinates easier. If Boxer were found guilty, there might be a chance the charges against the men would be dropped before they went to trial.

Admiral Walford, the senior and therefore the "President" of the court-martial board, turned to Boxer after the charges were read.

"The United States Navy asks you now defendant Admiral John Boxer . . . How do you plead . . . guilty or not guilty? You have also the option under the Uniform Code of standing mute. If that is the case, then a plea of Not Guilty must be assumed and entered on your behalf.

"Not Guilty," Boxer said, loud enough for all two hundred spectators to hear.

"The court will note that the defendant pleaded not guilty to all of the charges and specifications," the admiral said.

Rear Admiral Gaines proved to be a tough competitor. He had the timetable of the hijack of the SSN-S1 down to the minute. He had all of the details correct and a complete list of radio communication.

It was in the second day of the prosecution's side of the case that Gaines introduced evidence that made Boxer confer with Chase and consider a change in his status.

"If it please the court," Gaines said, "I wish to play and then enter into evidence the following tape monitored by STRATCOM units in Norfolk when the SSN-S1 was pirated."

"Have you objection to this, Counsel?" the president of the court asked Chase.

"The defense does not, sir."

"Very well." The president turned to the court clerk. "Mark it for identification and call it government exhibit seven."

Boxer turned to Chase. "If they let that in, we're sunk," he whispered.

"There are no grounds I can use to keep it out..It was an overheard radio communication. When you made that statement it was your hope that damn near everyone in the world *would* hear it. I think that damn near everyone in the world *did*. So, there is no keeping it out of court. The best you can hope to do is make something of it."

"That would mean I would have to testify."

"Your choice, Jack. If you do, you liable yourself to be cross-examined by Gaines."

"I guess I'll have to risk that. Maybe I can score some points with the board. You said we only have to convince two . . . right?"

Chase nodded.

It was a minute later when Gaines had a tape recorder brought into the court and the tape was played.

"To the people of the world, this is Admiral Jack Boxer aboard the American submarine SSN-1 . . . My crew and I have taken over this submarine in order to destroy a hot zone—a place created by unscrupulous men, who are involved in the disposal of nuclear waste. If this is not stopped, the oceans of the world will be contaminated, and your lives and life of the oceans will be at risk. This can not be allowed to happen. Once we succeed in destroying the hot zone, we will return, and demand that those accountable for the death of an entire crew of a Russian submarine be tried and punished.

"One last word, if we are fired upon, we will defend ourselves. It is not our purpose to seek hostile action, but to those who would try to stop us, I have only one word of advice: Don't."

Gaines turned to the members of the court. "There is no doubt that the man who identifies himself on the tape is the defendant. We have had the voice on the tape compared to other verified recordings of the defendant's voice and the results indicate that the voices match. We intend to enter this as government exhibit."

"Mister President and members of the court?" Chase was on his feet and Gaines, confused, yielded him the floor.

"Gentlemen, at this time my client wishes to indicate that he will take the stand on his own behalf and in his own defense."

The court agreed as did a baffled Rear Admiral Gaines, who had expected that Boxer was going to be silent for the entire trial. After all, the man had nothing to gain by taking the stand.

"State your name, rank, and last duty station," Chase asked.

"John Boxer, Rear Admiral, United States Navy, late commanding officer of the SSN-S1 specializing in salvage operations."

"Admiral Boxer, will you familiarize the members of the court with your service record? Perhaps you could enumerate the decorations that you wear on the left pocket of your uniform?"

"Very well, sir. From the top to the bottom, there would be a Navy Cross, a Silver Star Medal, a Bronze Star with three Oak Leaf Clusters and a "V" device on one of them. Then there is a Meritorious Service Medal and a Purple Heart with two Oak Leaf Clusters. There are campaign ribbons for service on *Yankee Station* in the

Vietnam War, service in support of Grenada, Panama, and Operation Desert Storm."

"And what are the ribbons on the right pocket, Admiral?"

"Oh," Boxer said. He was surprised that they had been mentioned. Chase was pulling out all of the stops.

"There is a Presidential Unit Citation with three clusters. And, there is a Meritorious Unit Citation. Then, there is a Vietnamese Cross of Gallantry and a Vietnamese Medal of Honor . . . the NATO Meritorious Service Medal. I think that's it, sir."

"And was the Navy Cross, Admiral Boxer . . . a downgraded medal? By that I mean, was it downgraded from a higher one for which you had been recommended?"

"Yes, sir."

"Can you tell the court what that decoration was, Admiral?"

"Yes, sir."

Gaines was on his feet before Chase could go any further.

"There is no need to enumerate the decorations that the defendant lays claim to. The government will readily accept there are a great many decorations here."

"Overruled," the president of the court scowled.

Boxer waited until the objection had been overruled. Chase smiled at the small victory.

"Once again, Admiral . . . the decoration that the Navy Cross had been substituted for?" Chase queried.

"The Congressional Medal of Honor, sir."

"And what were you cited for?"

"It was for a prisoner rescue action in the Vietnam War."

113

"It was, was it not, for an action that you initiated which resulted in the rescue of fifteen POWs held in a camp near the Nung River . . . is that correct?"

"Yes, sir, it is."

"And you devised this mission . . . is that correct?"

"I did, sir, with the help of a few others."

"What I mean to ask, Admiral Boxer, is that you carried out this action without the permission of superior officers, is that so?"

"We did, sir."

"And you were rewarded for it by being put in for the Congressional Medal of Honor. Right?"

"That's correct, sir."

"And, what would have happened if the mission had been a failure? If you had not gotten any of the prisoners out alive?"

"Objection. . . ." Gaines was on his feet. "That calls for a conclusion on the part of the defendant."

"Sustained," Admiral Walford said.

"Very well," Chase responded without missing a beat. "Let me put this another way. Admiral Boxer, did your superiors mention to you the eventuality if the mission had not been successful?"

"They did, sir."

"And, what did they say would happend to you, Admiral?"

Jack Boxer smiled a wry smile. "Sir, they said I would be facing a General Court-Martial."

There was a roar of laughter in the room.

Gaines's face reddened. He turned to his Assistant Trial Counsel and asked the young officer to make a note.

Admiral Walford gaveled the room back to silence.

He reached for the mike in front of him and cleared his throat before he spoke.

"This court-martial is sitting to hear charges that carry the potential of the death penalty for the accused. I suggest that we keep the noise to a minimum. If there are other outbursts, I will order the room cleared and I don't care how many members of the press are here."

There was a long moment of silence and Walford looked back to Chase. "You may continue, Counselor."

"I have no further questions."

Now it was Gaines's turn. He leafed through a handful of yellow pad pages before he turned to Boxer.

"Admiral, did you hear the tape entered into evidence as . . . government exhibit seven?"

"I did, sir."

"Was that your voice on the tape?"

"It was, sir."

"Did you steal the Submarine SSN-S1?"

"No, sir."

Gaines blinked. "Admiral, you admitted that the voice on the tape is yours. Correct?"

"That is correct, sir."

"If that is correct than how can you say you did not steal . . . pirate the SSN-S1?"

"I did not steal it, sir. I . . . borrowed it with the full intention of returning it to the United States Navy. Had I not been intercepted, I would have done exactly that."

"You are accused of piracy, Admiral. How do you expect us to believe that you were going to return the SSN-S1?"

"Sir, you played a tape of my voice stating the intentions of the mission. The objective was to destroy the hot zone in the North Pacific Ocean. The tape says once we have been successful, we would return. Your task force arrived before we could return the boat to Norfolk."

"Admiral Boxer, if you stole a hundred thousand dollars from a bank and said that you simply borrowed it with the full intention of returning it, would you be any less guilty of bank robbery?"

"I don't know, sir," Boxer said to the Trial Counsel with a smile. "I'm not a lawyer."

"I propose that it does not take a lawyer to answer that question, Admiral Boxer. Please answer it."

"I suspect I would be guilty."

"No further questions."

The four men filed in looking down. Boxer did not take it to be a good sign. They had been in session some five hours and Chase had told him that the length of time was not one he could get a "feel" from. If they had been out for fifteen minutes, the chances were excellent that he would have been guilty. Conversely, the chances improved for acquittal the longer the deliberation went.

"The accused will rise."

Boxer and Chase got to their feet.

"The court-martial by secret written ballot, two thirds of the members present at the time of the ballot finds you of all charges and specifications . . . guilty."

There was pandemonium in the court. Reporters headed for phones. Portapack cameras recorded. Boxer slipped back into his seat. He had expected it, especially after he had testified. What he had to sweat out now was the sentencing. It could be a slap on the wrist. Or . . . it could mean a hangman's rope.

* * *

It was a full three days before the court-martial returned with a sentence. Boxer stood with Chase and listened while the list of the charges was read. In a few minutes, which seemed to take hours, Admiral Walford paused and looked at Boxer.

"This court has had to weigh a great many factors in determining the nature of the punishment that should be meted out for this very serious crime. Among the factors given weight were the letters of commendation and the combat decorations awarded the defendant and his expressed motives for pirating the SSN-S1. It is the judgment of this court that the actions that have been proven here were not in any way undertaken for personal gain.

"Therefore, it is the sentence of this court that the defendant, Rear Admiral John Boxer, be dishonorably discharged from the United States Navy. In addition, he will pay a fine of one hundred thousand dollars as remuneration for damages done to government property. He will also forfeit all retirement pay, allowances and privileges now due or ever to come due. This court stands adjourned."

Boxer placed his hands palms down on the table in front of himself. For the first time in his adult life he felt like he was going to faint. The sentence was the lightest one that the court-martial board could ever have reasonably imposed. He had been spared the hangman's rope and the prison cell. He looked at the four men as they filed from the room and, for a split second, his eyes met Walford's. There was a slight hint of a smile on the old man's face. Boxer nodded imperceptibly.

They understood one another.

Chapter Nine

The Tibo Trough near Anu Roti is on the eastern end of the Java trench. The mountains of Surakarta rise in the distance and the sight of them was enough to keep the crew of the *Exxon Indonesia* ready for shore leave at any time.

The *"Ex-Ind"* as the crew called her was the mother ship and umbilicus tender for the seafloor drilling rig called simply and unimaginatively, the *SF1*. Essentially, Captain George Lancaster found the work boring. But, there was no question that the money was good . . . better for those breathing heli-ox in a tin can a thousand feet down on an escarpment. Boring it might be, he thought but without the umbilicus and the provisions of the mother ship *Ex-Ind,* the *SF1* would die a quick death.

Captain Lancaster looked across the slake blue water. It was smooth as glass, not a ripple, nor a breeze. It was typical of equatorial latitudes in the morning. Later, there would be a breeze from the northwest. It was one of the trade winds that blew sailing ships through the East Indies more than five hundred years ago. But, just now, the temperature was ninety-five and rising. It was close to midsummer in the tropics and until the trade winds rose, the heat would be oppressive. Lancaster thanked his stars for air conditioning. He reminded himself to tell his Exec that the watch crews should all wear sunscreen and hats. Sun poisoning could be acquired in less than an hour in these latitudes.

The 6:00 A.M. watch had just gone on duty when the *SF1* coma line buzzed.

The duty officer took the call and after a moment turned to the captain.

"Sir, it's Bill Fergusson."

Lancaster thought it odd that Fergusson should call so early. The seafloor rig, in permanent darkness, was keyed to the schedule of the *Ex-Ind* on the surface. It was helpful for record-keeping purposes to have both rigs on the same schedule. But, Fergusson was not due to send a sit-rep up until 9:00 A.M. He was three hours early. It was not like Bill. Lancaster moved his mental alert systems up a notch.

"Morning, Bill. What can we do for you?"

"Morning, George. I don't want to appear jumpy, but with all the weird stuff going on around here recently, I want to make sure that I report everything. I'm sure you know what I mean."

"What you're saying is you want to cover your fanny, right?"

"I guess so."

"So whacha got? A mermaid?"

"I have an intermittent sonar contact at about three thousand yards. But, she's above us and on the far

119

side of a heavyside layer. It's as if she's using it to hide. You know what I mean?"

"I read you. What's the size of the target? Can you get an approximate on it?"

"Computer says a single high-speed screw. Teardrop configuration. She makes high-speed revs."

"Sure as shit not a whale. Is it, Bill?"

There was a long pause and a few stabs of static on the line.

"Lancaster to Fergusson. Do you read me?"

Nothing.

"Lancaster to Fergusson. I say again . . . do you read me?"

"I'll be a son of a bitch."

"Bill! What the hell's going on?" There was clear tension and a bit of annoyance in Lancaster's voice now. Indeed, there *had* been too many incidents lately. Everyone was jumpy.

"Fergusson to Lancaster. The target seems to be a Soviet *Alfa* class attack submarine, cruising at about the top layer of the heavyside. Depth about five hundred feet I'd say."

"Bill, I'm taking no chances with this. Stay on the line."

Lancaster switched from the radio to the loudspeaker and intercom. His voice reached every compartment and deck space of the *Ex-Ind*.

"This is the captain. Security Alert. Security vessels prepare to get under way. Initiate Plan ECHO. I say again, initiate Plan ECHO. Out."

Lancaster flipped a switch on the handset and was again on the radio.

"Bill, I scrambled the two minisubs. They'll be away in five minutes and be at the target in five more. Hold One." Again, he moved the handset position to another setting.

"Sonar! Get me a fix based on Fergusson's estimated position."

"Aye, aye, sir." The answer spat back out of the speaker.

It took only a few seconds to acquire the target.

"Sonar, Captain. I have the target. She is difficult to track. Her position is almost directly below us and above the *SF1*. She slips in and out of the heavyside and she's hard to hold as a target. The minis should get her, though. They can triangulate if they approach from different angles."

"Keep me informed, Enrico. I want to know if she twitches."

"Do the best I can, sir. It's worth mentioning, sir, that she is close to the umbilicus."

"Acknowledged, Enrico. Keep on him."

In a second, Lancaster was back on the radio to the *SF1*.

"Bill, do you read?"

"Roger."

"Sonar says that the bogey is close to the umbilicus. I think you should go Alert. Get your off-duty personnel in their pods and consider this as a real threat. I estimate that we have three minutes to the launch of the minis. I want to be ready if this son of a bitch wants trouble."

"What are the minis carrying?"

"Two Mark XX's and a Sea Dart apiece."

"Yeah. A missile exchange at that range from the umbilicus would tear up the pea patch all right. For the record, we are going to Alert and per instructions I am ordering all off-duty personnel into escape apparatus."

His comments were specifically meant for recording on an audio tape that transcribed all transmitted orders and monitored all meaningful exchanges on the bridge. Like the flight recorders on aircraft, the tape was present to offer up explanations in case of catastrophe . . . and an alibi if anyone survived. While both men hoped such an event was not in the cards, they could not be sure considering the madness of the recent attacks on Java rigs.

A Soviet *Alfa,* Lancaster thought. What the hell would something like that be doing here? It was one of their most advanced attack boats back when there had been a Red Navy. She was one of the most sophisticated subs in the world and if she were hostile, would prove a wily adversary.

"Mini-A to conn. Feet are wet. Diving to bogey position."

The Mini-A commander was a former Annapolis instructor in undersea tactics named Pasani who had seen the end of his Navy career with the end of the Cold War. He left his intercom open to feed the same tape as the others.

"Mini-A to B. Move to the flank. Acknowledge."

"Mini-B. That's a Roger." Ensign Zeke Caldwell's Alabama drawl hid his lightning reflexes and expertise with the minisub. He had been through the Kings Point Merchant Marine Academy. He, too, was one of the best at this kind of thing. Pasani and Caldwell had spent a lot of hours in simulators as well as in the minis, preparing for a contingency like they now faced. They had been ordered to the rig at the outset of violence in the region, and they had been training ever since.

"Mini-B to Conn . . . I have a make. She's an *Alfa* all right. Low sail . . . teardrop configuration and a single screw. Who the hell is running the son of a bitch?"

BONNNGGG!

"What the fuck?" Caldwell yelled into the headset mike. "I just got a directional sonar ping. Pounded the shit out of me. I'm getting told to back off . . . I think."

BONNNNGGGG!

"I just got one, too," Pasani echoed. "We're both zeroed. Mini-A to conn. Call it war of nerves time. This guy is up to no good. Request permission to arm weapons?"

Lancaster had to think and there was no time. Would arming the weapons provoke the *Alfa?* Would it frighten them away? He couldn't know. He took a chance.

"Permission to arm granted."

On the floor of the trough, Fergusson was already upgrading his readiness status and leaving his mike open to record it.

"Sound collision alarm."

"Collision alarm, aye." The crewman slammed at a stud on a panel in front of him. A Klaxon started to sound. Yellow lights flashed.

"Close all watertight doors. Establish independent pressure."

"Stand clear all watertight doors!" The taped announcement repeated itself five times before the doors started to close.

"Green board on WTD closing completed." The electronics were telling the console operator that the doors were dogged and holding pressure. The last step was to build independent air pressure in each of the separated pressure. As each had integrity, they might survive an implosion if they were semiautonomous units. Theoretically, the thinking was fine . . . though Exxon had never really used the system in an actual emergency. "Pressure build completed. And collision prep completed. Conn."

"Very well," Fergusson commented almost absently. The actions had been carried out so frequently in drill situations that they had become automatic.

"George . . . we're buttoned up. Acknowledge."

"Roger that, *SF1*," Lancaster said looking at the TV camera shot of the *Alfa*, which was precariously close to the umbilicus.

BONNNGG!

"He hit me again," Pasani reported.

A second later, Caldwell also was hit.

Lancaster brought the mike close to his lips. "Could be a response to you arming your systems. He has to know you did. A mackerel couldn't shit a hundred miles away without that *Alfa*'s gear catching it."

"Skipper?" Pasani queried. "If he's going to launch an attack he has to have already assessed our defense capability. If he launches first, the *Ex-Ind* has no de-

124

fenses at all. Nor does the *SF1*. Our defense in this situation is to be offensive; make him defend against us. So, I request permission to engage."

"The company says we can't fire first, remember?"

"Company ain't here. They're back at their stateside desks, remember?"

"*Alfa's* flooded tubes. I say again, he's flooded tubes," Caldwell screamed.

"Let me engage . . . now, Lancaster. He's gonna whack us. I just know it. I have a solution already in the computer."

"His outer doors are coming open," Caldwell screamed. "For Christ's sake, let us engage."

It was Lancaster's sonar operator who made the decision for him.

"Small transients close aboard. Torpedo launched. Torpedo is searching. Torpedo has acquired."

The man pulled his headset off and looked to the wing bridge where Lancaster waited with the mike in his hand.

"We are the target. I say again, we are the target. Estimated time to impact . . . forty seconds. Thirty-nine . . . thirty-eight. . . ."

"Engage! Engage!" Lancaster screamed into the mike.

"Engaging," Caldwell and Pasani chimed together. Both launched noisemakers and ECM signals to scramble the homing servos that were guiding the torpedo to the *Ex-Ind*.

They also both launched American made Mark XX homing torpedoes. Both immediately sought the target and closed.

The *Alfa* immediately went to flank speed and launched her own countermeasures.

The seas filled with electronic signals and counter signals. All Lancaster could do was hope that some of it managed to fool relentless computer on the torpedo that had locked onto them.

"Twenty-one . . . twenty. . . ."

On the bottom, Fergusson was preparing to launch his life pods with the crew members. He was sure that once the mother ship was gone, he would be the target.

"Sixteen . . . fifteen. . . ." The sonar man's voice did not waver.

Lancaster squinted off to the sea as if to see a wake or some indication of the torpedo. "Any change in aspect?"

"Negative. Twelve seconds . . . eleven. . . ."

"Sound the collision alarm."

"Roger," the sonarman snapped and the Klaxons started to scream everywhere.

"Launching Sea Darts," Pasani snapped.

"Four . . . three. . . ."

The Soviet made torpedo penetrated the underside of the *Ex-Ind* and travelled upward into the engine room for more than a second and a half before the proximity fuse detonated the two-ton H.E. charge.

The bottom two decks of the *Ex-Ind* ceased to exist. Ranging upward in the first split second, the fireball flashed through the fuel bunkers and ignited. The ensuing explosion blew huge sections of deckplate from the upper deck and killed seventy-five of the eighty crewmen. Lancaster was blown from the wing bridge into the water some forty feet below.

In less than a minute, the more than seven-hundred-foot-long *Ex-Ind* was awash with flames and was sinking fast. The torpedo hit had been perfect — for a quick kill. It impacted at the dead center of the keel; its penetration power was akin to an armor piercing shell forcing deep into the recesses of the tank before going off.

Lancaster came to the surface coughing and sputtering. All that remained of the ship he had commanded less than a minute ago was a sinking super structure, a fiery pool, and bubbling froth. He tread water for a few minutes watching the fire burn. A large piece of dunnage lumber from somewhere deep in one of the holds bobbed to the surface. Lancaster started to swim for it, but as he started the stroke he felt the pain.

His back had been slammed into the water and was badly wrenched. The shock was just starting to wear off and Lancaster was beginning to feel it. He managed to pull himself onto the makeshift raft of dunnage timber. The effort of pulling himself on top of the wood was exhausting. He lay on his back until he caught his breath. A few minutes later he pushed himself to his feet and looked at what had once been the *Ex-Ind*. The burning oil pyre was all that was left.

Here and there he could see figures in the water; most of them did not move. He watched with regret and despair. Did none of his crew survive? Amazingly, two of them did. He could see their shapes yelling and waving.

He recognized only one of the two. It was Enrico.

He was blackened with soot but seemed to swim strongly in the direction of the captain. The other man started to fall behind; in a minute or two, Lancaster lost track of him. Lancaster actually managed a smile. For a long moment in the water he thought he had been the only survivor. It would have been too much to bear. He looked across the dunnage pile to find something to help Enrico aboard.

There was nothing.

With his back pain increasing every minute, Lancaster managed to get to his knees and prepare to help Enrico aboard.

Enrico was thirty or forty yards from the safety of the lumber pile when Lancaster saw the dorsal fin cutting the water behind the swimmer. It rose nearly two feet from the surface and there was a space of nearly ten feet from the dorsal to the tall fin. It was moving so fast that it created a bow wave.

Only one fish in the world did that . . . a Great White.

"Enrico, faster . . . behind you." Lancaster gestured frantically, but Enrico either didn't hear or understand what the gestures meant.

The fin of the Great White moved faster as it cut the distance between itself and Enrico.

Lancaster screamed and waved with both hands.

Now, only twenty yards from the safety of the makeshift raft, Enrico turned his head and caught a flash of the fin. He frantically increased his pace.

As he increased speed, the dorsal dipped below the surface of the water. The Great White had spun onto its back.

Enrico was only eight yards from Lancaster's out-stretched hand; the dazed captain reached as far out from the side as he safely could.

They were only feet apart when the Great White struck.

Enrico was instantly pulled under. A swirl of foam turned pink, then red. For a split second, Lancaster could see what he thought was a leg near the raft. Then it, too, vanished in the red foam.

He fell on his back and looked at the blazing sun. He cried.

An enormous fist slammed into the *SF1*, shaking it violently.

"*Ex-Ind* . . . Acknowledge." Fergusson yelled into the mike, while holding onto a stanchion for support. The dying lights and sudden loss of signal and other "feeds" from the surface hinted at what he did not want to hear.

In a matter of seconds, battery and back-up generator systems tripped and the rig was working at almost the same level as it had been before the stoppage.

"COMMO, keep trying to get the *Ex-Ind*. Sonar, what have we got?"

The sonarman pressed the headset to his ears.

"Surface clutter. Hard to wash it." His hands played across the computer controls that slipped various frequencies of sound out of the sonar picture.

"Oh shit!"

"What is it?" Fergusson barked.

"*Ex-Ind* is gone, sir. Looks like she took a fish.

That was the surface clutter. She's gone, but we're in the shit now."

"How, sonar?"

"The *Ex-Ind*, sir."

"I know. She's sunk. You just said that. What do you mean?"

"That's what I said. The *Ex-Ind*, sir. She *is* sunk. Precisely . . . she is sinking . . . right on top of us. That was what I got when I washed the surface clutter."

Fergusson slammed a switch on the intercom. A Klaxon started its nerve-wracking litany.

"Collision alarm! Collision alarm! Prepare to abandon rig. Pre—"

Bong!

A large piece of heavy metal ricocheted off the top of the rig's pressure hull. It was the first drop in a metal rainstorm. In a matter of seconds pieces of the *Ex-Ind* were pummeling the pressure domes and bouncing away.

Fergusson had to scream to make himself heard in the din.

"Where is the rest of the hull? Where is the main body of the ship?" He was trying to determine if he had time to get the crew off in the "coffins" before the rainstorm became fatal. If he did not have time, all he could hope for was that the currents were kind.

"Close," Sonar shouted. "Very close . . . almost too close to measure." He reached out and turned up the column on the active sonar ping. The range to the falling wreckage was shortening.

PaaaaaaaaaPing . . . PaaaaPing . . . PaaaPing . . .

Paaping . . . Papingpapingpa. . . .

The crash of screaming metal cut off the sonar beep. The lights winked out in the rig and alarm bells clanged in all of the spaces. Pressure had been lost somewhere in the rig.

Emergency lights flickered on.

Fergusson had managed to keep on his feet by keeping his grip on the stanchion.

"Damage control. Get me a report as soon as possible. Also, I need visual on the outside of the rig. How wrapped up are we?"

He looked to his right where a large bubble port showed him that wreckage from the dead surface whip was festooned on almost all of the surfaces. Also, the rig had seemingly pulled free of her drilling pipe. She was free in a number of ways . . . tied neither to the well or the surface.

Bill Fergusson tried to plot the position of the wreckage in his head but he knew that he was going to have to have people in minis out there to plot it for him. As long as he had wreckage coming down, there was no chance to launch a scout to explore his damage. His predicament was similar to a doctor doing heart surgery by feel alone. It clearly cut down on his options. "Damage control report," a voice on the intercom said. There was fear in the voice.

"Very well." Fergusson tried to sound calm though he knew know no one in his crew really would believe him.

"Sir, we have collapse damage in pods three and seventeen." Fergusson knew that the announcement meant that any men on those pods were dead, crushed by millions of tons of seawater.

But, Fergusson wanted to hold off that part of the news. He would rather get the information on the damage to the structure.

"What else have we got?"

Again, there was a trace of fear in the voice.

"We have compression loss in chambers eleven and fourteen. We have electrical failure in seventeen of the escape pods and this one is the worst, Skipper. The heli-ox operation is damaged. We have something on the order of five and a half hours of reserve heli-ox mix."

The sound of the man's voice was a death knell. The pressure of a thousand feet of seawater was sufficient to press the dissolved nitrogen in the bloodstream into bubbles that pooled at the joints. The disease was called Nitrogen Narcosis but was more commonly called the "bends." Helium and oxygen mixed provided the deep diving crew with an environment that prevented the bubbling and allowed them to work. The downside of this environment was the fact that in order to adjust down to the depth or back to topside, everyone had to decompress . . . make a slow adjustment to the surface pressure and the normal mix of nitrogen rather than helium with oxygen. If the H-O mixing apparatus was damaged, not only did the rig need rescue in five hours, but whoever came to rescue them had to have a large capacity for decompression. Luckily, a number of rigs in the Java strike had such facilities. Fergusson clung to the hope with desperate tenacity.

"Can we launch the pod?"

"Roger."

"Launch it then," Fergusson ordered.

The pods were automated beacons with small, powerful transmitters keyed to Navstar coordinates. Satellites were keyed to the signals and would react by passing the alert to the other company vessels in the area. In turn, these crafts would hopefully send help which included decompression chambers.

"Pods away, sir."

"Very well. Have we got communications?"

"Just jury-rigging the 'Granny' together now, sir. We have a signal from the minisubs, sir. Not sure if we can transmit yet. But, I know we can receive."

"What's going on out there?" Fergusson asked.

"Boosting volume."

There was a flare of static and the chatter between Pasani and Caldwell was suddenly intelligible.

"Have you got 'im? Have you got 'im?" Caldwell was shouting.

"Target aspect is changing," responded the calmer voice of Pasani. "He's turning. Mini-two launch your weapons now . . . now . . . now."

"Launching," Caldwell answered.

In the distance and a hundred fifty fathoms above, the two minis were trying to triangulate the position of the *Alfa*. They wanted to get off two torpedoes at the same time knowing that the *Alfa* would have difficulty in evading two of them at once. Noisemakers and ECM could take care of one torpedo computer but two at a time was too much of a challenge. All Bill Fergusson could do . . . was listen.

"Torpedo away. Torpedo has acquired." Caldwell's

voice was strident. He was frightened but, Fergusson thought, not as frightened as me.

"Mine's away, too," Pasani called into his mike. "Seeking . . . Yes! Acquired."

Both Mark XX torps were moving in the direction of the target. They were on their own . . . two idiot computers seeing a target and directing their servo mechanisms to change course as the target shifted position.

The *Alfa* had more than a turn of speed on the minis and it had a greater range of weapons. Each of them carried only two of the Mark XXs and it was certain that their renegade *Alfa* had a couple of dozen torpedoes and missiles at her disposal.

"They're both running hot," Pasani yelled.

Fergusson found himself silently cheering the actions of the minisub skippers. The survival of him and his men on the crippled rig depended on them in large measure.

"Confirm both running hot," Caldwell said.

Suddenly, the *Alfa* did the unexpected.

"It's an emergency blow," Caldwell yelled.

Fergusson knew enough about subs to know this meant that the *Alfa* was heading for the surface as fast as she could. In the wash of bubbles, there was a chance that she could confuse one or perhaps both of the torpedoes.

"Torp One is veering off," Pasani shouted. The first of the torpedoes had gotten confused. It only took another second for the second torp to follow. The emergency blow was a stroke of genius on the part of the *Alfa* skipper, whoever he was.

"Multiple transients. I make it four . . . no . . . six. All seeking," Caldwell intoned. He knew what it meant. The *Alfa* had counterattacked. She had managed to get a full spread of fish in the water as she rose through the curtain of her bubbles. Unlike the torps of the minis, hers were wire guided. Their shortened range was compensated for by their deadly accuracy.

"I've been zeroed," Pasani called into his mike more for the record than anything else. Fergusson could feel his heart sink as he listened.

"They have me, too," Caldwell yelled. "Think it's time to get the hell out of here."

Both men ejected in their self-contained escape pods which slowly made for the surface.

Listening, Fergusson wished he could do the same. But, the submariners were not using heli-ox. There was no decompression problem for them. The pods that the *SF1* would launch would have to be "processed" through decompression for more than a day before the men inside could emerge.

"Sonar, Skipper."

"What is it?" Fergusson asked, already half knowing.

"We're being sonar probed. Small signal but steady. Acts like a torp." The sonar operator had not heard the exchange between the two sub drivers. In a matter of seconds he would feel the concussion of the hits that would demolish the minis. Then . . . he would know.

But, Fergusson could not allow them to wait that long. If there were to be a chance for his men at all, it would have to be floating on the surface in the pods that were perhaps well nicknamed "coffins."

"Abandon rig. I say . . . abandon rig."

In a matter of seconds, he would hear the compressed air scream as the few remaining undamaged pods were ejected.

It was only a second or two before Fergusson heard the scream of the torpedo engine as it bore relentlessly in through the wreckage of the *Ex-Ind* to detonate and totally implode the *SF1*.

Chapter Ten

Eric Von Stempler watched as the high summer clouds slipped through the upper reaches of the Alpine passes and dropped near the surface of the Zurichsee. *Krieg* was going perfectly. The three *Alfas* had been well worth the incredible price he had to pay when they were mothballed from the now bankrupt CIS Navy. Thanks to the work of the *Krieg* team, recruited through Libya and comprised of the best outcasts of the world's navies, the Java strike area had been decimated and the Middle East oil holdings of the World Wide Disposal Corporation had grown fat, indeed. There were problems to be wrestled with, still.

Igor Borodine was fighting bureaucratic red tape in Moscow and Admiral Jack Boxer was officially out of the United States Navy and in disgrace, they could not touch him. The problem he faced was a long-range one and it concerned exposure rather than anything else.

Quite simply, he was going to have to find a way to get rid of the *Krieg* crews and support staffs. They knew more than enough to hang him in any court in the world. And, given the men that they were, any of them would betray him to save themselves, despite the money he was paying them.

He could only moan about the loyalty that had been lost since his father, a Nazi *Oberst,* had rolled his utterly obedient men and their powerful *panzers* through the Russian steppes. Well, he thought, those days are gone and will not return. What has to be used nowadays to simulate fidelity is high tech strategies.

He pressed a button on a console at the top of his desk. A woman's voice answered cheerily. "Yes, Herr Von Stempler?"

"Send the good Herr Doktor in."

It took only a minute for the man to come in. He was plain, drab, and paunchy. He was in his fifties wearing a ten-year-old suit that strained at the waist from a diet that screamed of wurst and beer. Doktor Professor Heinreich Von Kleist from Goethe Universität in Frankfurt was perhaps the most skilled man in the world in the area of the relatively new field of Bio-Systems Engineering. He had been on the payroll of the WWDC, AG., for over a year and had been integrally involved in the training of the crews.

"Come in, Herr Doktor. Please sit down."

The frumpy man slouched in the offered seat.

"Now, Heinreich, if I may call you that . . . ?"

"Of course," the intimidated small man intoned.

"As I was saying, I did not have the time to discuss the project as thoroughly as I would have liked when we were getting things together. Please give me the briefing. I know this matter can get rather complicated."

"Yes, well, I'll do my best. Conditioning cycles, both audio and visual, have been used to program large portions of the population for a long time. It's a direct feed to the subconscious. The first experiments in this influence, for want of a better word, were done in the fifties when chains of movie houses would use a frame with a picture of popcorn and a message that said, eat popcorn, on the screen in every hundredth frame or so. That was the beginning. While there are minor regulations governing the use of the subliminal audio and subliminal visual techniques in the United States and several other countries, few of them are enforced. Most countries didn't really know that the technique existed."

Von Stempler was trying to maintain his patience. He was a man with such rare, spare time that he truly had no time to hear or read anything more than summaries or capsules of information. He was, though, starting to find the frumpy man's words . . . interesting.

"So, the subjects believe that they are undergoing a loyalty test with a scan for subconscious problems. Actually, they are undergoing a preliminary hypnotic exam to see if they are good subjects. If the three were good subjects, we take them through the larger conditioning sequence. In it, we program them to reinforce the initial hypnotic sequence. By the time they finish the sequence, they are ready to carry out any command that is in the last of the sequenced tapes."

"How are the tapes gotten to them?"

The Doktor Professor smiled, revealing gnarled teeth. "I am most proud of that, Herr Von Stempler.

The tapes were all on the submarines before they left port. However, to any but the conditioned person, they would only be music tapes and not very interesting, given the musical tastes of the sailors in Task Force *Krieg*."

"But, you are sure it will work when we transmit this . . . what do you call it? Trigger signal?"

"The odds are heavily in favor of complete success. What happens is that the subject is instructed to listen to the operative tape before he is to go on watch or duty again. The trigger tumbles a mental set of instructions that have been hiding, so to speak, in the man's subconscious since the initial interview. What the man will do is destroy the control rod servos and start a runaway meltdown in the sub's reactor. He will then flood the boat. Between the seawater and the radiation, all of the crew will be . . . accounted for."

"Dead men tell no tales?"

"Exactly, sir."

"What if there has been a malfunction in the equipment?"

"Sir, the odds against that are very great indeed. Of course, no system is utterly foolproof. These men are in combat and there are stress factors that we cannot account for. However, suffice it to say that the three men . . . officers actually . . . are in positions on each of the *Alfas* that allow them to have access to any part of the sub. When they activate the last programming tape it will be a natural event . . . like another tape in a selection of educational tapes that they have brought on board. Once the last tape is played and they listen to it, there is little chance that they cannot carry out

140

the sequence that will result in the destruction of the sub."

The frumpy German folded his hands in his lap; he was more than a little pleased with himself.

"Well, when that is accomplished, Herr Doktor, I will insure that the funds we have discussed will be deposited in your account."

"Thank you, sir."

"There is only one thing that I find disconcerting."

"What is that, sir?"

"Well, we are dealing with self-preservation here. It is our most basic instinct. How can you short-circuit it? How can you make a man willing to walk into a nuclear reactor or do the equivalent of that?"

"Sir, a great deal of the conditioning has much to do with the earliest part of our brains that develop. It has to do with the part of the limbic system that deals with pleasure. Have you ever heard of the clinically valuable experiments with monkeys at Yale?"

Von Stempler smiled politely and shook his head.

"Well, a researcher established that the pleasure centers of the monkey's brains could be stimulated electrically and then he gave the monkeys buttons that could provide the stimulus. They were allowed to choose between the pleasure response and food."

"And, of course, they chose the pleasure response?"

"Absolutely. They pressed the buttons at the expense of food until they eventually starved to death. Sir, we are dealing with many of the same reflexes here. Self-preservation *can* be short-circuited."

"I believe you, Herr Doktor. It has been a pleasure speaking to you."

"Sir." The Doctor was on his feet and out the door in a matter of seconds.

Eric smiled after the door closed. The man was frightening and what he controlled was terrifying. It was the ultimate power and it should never be entrusted to someone as shortsighted as an academic scientist.

Eric determined that he would see to it that the Doktor Professor met with an unfortunate accident somewhere in Zurich before the need to pay him became something to be dealt with.

In the hall, Herr Doktor Von Kleist was sure what he was feeling was right. The man who had endowed his research was not to be trusted. There was a good chance his "benefactor" meant to kill him and take all of his techniques and use them for himself.

Well, he thought, there are a great many ways to deal with such threats. Some of them could involve the kinds of techniques he was researching. He could turn the fire against the fireman. Yes, he could, he thought.

He smiled and pressed the button for the elevator.

Chapter Eleven

Olsen looked across the large desk to the President in the Oval Office and he tried to keep his voice somber. "There are nine attacks in the Java strike, sir, and our analysis indicates they are being carried out by one or more renegade subs that we can only assume are representatives of international terrorism. The price per barrel of oil is—"

"I know what the price is. I know damn well what the price is, Harry. The price is my re-election and the loss of both Houses of Congress to the opposition. It would be a defeat the like of which the party would not have seen in fifty years. All . . . over oil twelve thousand miles away."

Well, the President thought as he viewed the front lawn, am I going to have to do it? He could find no way around it.

"Harry . . . I want you to contact a man and arrange a meeting."

Boxer walked alone on the beach watching the flooding tide wipe out his footprints. Wiping out a career, he thought. No matter how cynical he had become in the last years of his Navy career, he had always managed to carry a small spark of patriotism somewhere deep in his gut.

Now, even the spark was threatened. Perhaps the spark was gone . . . like the footprints. Boxer tried to probe inside to find what was left, but he could find only darkness and confusion. All his life he had believed in *Carpe Diem!* Seize the Day! He took the initiative as often as possible. Now, there was little initiative to take. Over thirty years of his life was washed out in a few words of a sentence. He realized that he should feel grateful to the "Annapolis old boy circuit" for keeping him out of prison. He knew he also had to thank Carol Benson. Part of his mind set itself to prepare a special thanks for her. But, he could not find joy in the thought of her near him . . . not at this moment. Now , . . there was the beach and the taste of ashes.

"Can you stand some company?" Stark asked as he came up beside Boxer.

Boxer smiled. "I didn't hear you and I didn't see you. Am I losing it or what?"

"You're allowed. You've had a rough time recently. It's not something that you can bounce back from right away. I understand that . . . at least I think I do."

"All I can feel is emptiness and anger."

"The anger is healthy, Jack. I feel it, too. You want to get the sons of bitches that killed Kate and the others . . . who created the hot zone . . . the ones who set you up. But, perhaps there is a suggestion I can make."

"I hope it's for revenge."

"I don't think so. But, who can say?"

"I know you too well. You have something up your sleeve. Well, go ahead and explain. I can't see that it would do any harm."

Stark smiled and fell into step with his onetime student and consistent subordinate. "What I see is a salvage company, one that the Navy would have to come to for the very large jobs and one that would be able to do the jobs that the Navy could not take on by themselves."

"What kind of jobs?"

Stark shrugged. "Stuff below a thousand feet. Stuff that would need the new liquid breathers and a very sophisticated sub to run the operations."

"Seawolf class?" Boxer asked. His interest was starting to increase and Stark could see it.

"Of course. There's no other class that could do the deep work and manage to control the actions of a minisub. Of course, her Sherwood Forest would have been removed and replaced with docking bays for the minis and a moonpool for the access and egress of the suited divers. She could get down into the deep-sea trenches and get to the wrecks that the US and the Russkies gave up on long ago."

Boxer thought of the U-238 and the tons of Russian gold that were buried in her bowels at the bottom of the South China Sea. She was only one of the things that the joint CIS and American navies

145

would want to get their hands on now that the Cold War was over. There was a great deal of money and technology to be recovered there.

"Okay. I'm getting a hard-on. Tell me more you silver-tongued devil."

Stark leaned back and started to laugh. It grew into a belly laugh that Boxer had to join. The clouds seemed to clear from his soul for a moment.

"We set up a limited partnership and get some investors . . . all retired Navy of course. I already have one investor lined up. He has just put in his retirement papers. Good man . . . old sub driver."

"Do I know him?"

"You might. Name's Walford."

Boxer stopped in his tracks.

"You son of a bitch!"

"Calm yourself, Jack, m'boy. This is business."

"Of all the officers in the Navy, you had to get him involved in this? Jesus H. Christ, why couldn't you have found someone . . . anyone else?"

"For a couple of very good reasons, Jack. And, you have to hear them. There was a string rumor that in the court-martial board there had been at least one man who had been bought by an outside agency. It was set up for you to be found guilty and get the rope or at best the rest of your life in a naval prison."

"So, how did you ferret out that information? Walford?"

"Absolutely. Sometime before the convening of the court-martial. Did you think I was sitting down here

146

with my fingers up my ass waiting for you to be hanged, you stupid shit? Don't answer that.

"Anyway, I managed to get Walford in a position where he was the senior remaining officer after all of the challenges from Bill Chase and the Trial Counsel. It was a foregone conclusion they would find you guilty. Your conduct of the defense was good but not lawyer good and you know it."

Boxer was forced to nod. He turned and walked as Stark talked. They were heading back in the direction of Stark's house.

"So, the question was how far down the ladder in matters of extenuation and mitigation we could drive the sentence. A DD was about as low as they could go and still not look like they were stacking the deck."

"And part of the deal was a buy-in from Walford? Did you finance it?"

"None of your business, Jack. Boy, you sure are one fucking bull in a china shop when it comes to dealing with folks who are trying to help you. Can you shut up and listen?"

Boxer raised a hand in mock surrender as he walked. He *would* listen.

"There was not a man on that board who didn't sympathize with you in one way or another. Walford himself was the review authority on three or four of your fitness reports . . . in case you don't remember."

"He was?" Boxer asked, surprised.

"How can a normally bright man be so dense? Yes, he was. I managed to circulate the word

147

through the 'old boy circuit' that I was starting the operation and Walford came to me. That was after the court-martial had found you guilty and sentenced you. He told me he had his retirement papers in and asked if he could buy-in. I wondered what made him retire and he said he was tired of seeing men of your caliber beaten down by a system that had stopped being Navy some time ago. You don't get a much higher compliment than that, Jack. When I told him that you were going to be a part of the operation he said he was tickled and would up the ante on his investment. Said he would also talk to a few other Navy retirees . . . all flag types and see if he could recruit them."

"And, he did?"

"Yup. Almost didn't have to use any of my own money at all. A lot of those old sea dogs will be able to steer us in the direction of stuff that they couldn't really pursue when they were on active duty."

"And you want me to run this operation?"

"Would I be talking to you about it if I didn't?"

"We'd need a crew for that *Seawolf* boat and the right professionals to train them in the new technology. They'd have to train me, too, for that matter. There is a lot to stay current on. Is there a chance to get some of the old crew. The ones they let stay in the Navy wouldn't have much chance at advancement with a court-martial behind them."

Stark stopped at the bottom steps that led to the house via the large rear deck. "I've managed to recruit about twenty of them. Billingsly as chief of the boat . . . Sarkis, of course. Oh, and. . . ." He paused. The wind had shifted and so had the music from the huge stereo that Stark had in his living room. He had started to walk on the beach with the sounds of Jerome Kern wafting from the enormous speakers. Somehow, another compact disc had taken its place. He was listening to music he distantly recognized. But, it was certainly not Jerome Kern. It was not American. He distantly remembered . . . Prokofiev . . . yes, that's who it was. But, it wasn't *Peter and the Wolf* or something simple like that. It was something more symphonic.

"I know that's Prokofiev . . . but I can't place which," Boxer said. "I didn't know your tastes ran to Russian music," he added.

Stark shrugged. "I'm acquiring a taste for it. If I remember correctly that chorus is 'Arise ye Russian People,' from *Alexander Nevsky* . . . hell of an Eisenstein film. Ever see it?"

Boxer shook his head. "A bit too esoteric for me, I'm afraid."

"I always thought that of you, Admiral. Too bad."

Boxer looked to the top of the stairs and there stood Igor Borodine.

Boxer galloped up the stairs and shook hands with the man who had for so many years been his adversary and now had become such a close friend.

"Igor . . . how the hell are you? When Ilia said you had gone back to Moscow, I thought we would never see you again . . . especially when I heard that the man you were trying to ferret out had been

149

killed. I thought, well, I thought a lot of things. Now . . . I'm just glad you're here."

"Thank Stark for my being here. I thought if I was going to see you after I extricated myself from those Moscow bureaucrats, I'd have to go to a naval prison where you would be rotting for the rest of your life."

Boxer turned to Stark. "You put this all together. You are incredible, Admiral."

"I know," Stark said, without batting an eye.

Everyone broke into gales of laughter.

They were into their second round of drinks when Borodine moved the subject to his search for Tosenko.

"He had been a minor bureaucrat in the old Soviet mission to the United States. But he also had been a part of the Soviet mission to Germany and Switzerland. He had a lot of trade mission experience. He apparently had a special affinity for business dealings with a large conglomerate called WWD . . . that's World Wide Disposal Corporation."

"Where have I heard that name before?" Boxer asked, rhetorically.

"Among the connections that they seem to have had with the old Soviet regime was the disposal of spent nuclear reactor material."

"The hot zone?" Boxer asked.

"Quite possibly. There is no sure evidence, of course. But, the very fact that Tosenko was poisoned when I was making an attempt to contact him says something about the information he must have had.

150

There are a few facts that I have found that give me some leads."

"Don't stop now," Boxer said, pouring the Russian another drink.

"The man was killed with shellfish toxin. It seems that someone was in his apartment in New York, where the body was found. The autopsy seems to have revealed that the toxin was introduced through the skin by a pin prick. Someone got close to him and simply jabbed him."

"It would have to have been someone he knew," Stark added.

"Yes," Boxer commented. "He sounds like he would have been a careful man. A man like that would not let too many people near him . . . at least not that close."

"Perhaps a woman managed to get near him."

The voice was female and it came from the doorway to the deck.

It was Carol Benson.

The three men came to their feet . . . with Boxer the most surprised.

"Jack, I believe you've met Ms. Benson. Igor has met her earlier. I think you all met back on the *America.*"

"Yes," Boxer said, his eyes never leaving Carol. Here was the woman whose stories and editorials had slashed at the Navy for court-martialing him . . . castigating them for a massive miscarriage of justice. And what a stunning woman she was!

She wore a white sleeveless cocktail dress which

151

set off her long auburn hair and striking blue eyes. The clinging dress revealed the lines of her flawless breasts. Boxer could just see the outlines of nipples pressing themselves against the fabric. He found himself getting excited.

"C-Carol, I have you to thank for a great many things," he muttered, not able to find the right words.

"Not really. The set of columns I wrote did a lot to further my career. In fact, they were directly responsible for me getting the best job I've ever gotten."

"What's that?" Boxer asked, falling for the bait.

"Didn't Admiral Stark tell you, Jack?" she asked, half teasing and at the same time knowing that the admiral had mentioned nothing.

Boxer was utterly perplexed.

"Okay. I *am* an idiot. What haven't I been told? I know Stark loves to do this kind of stuff."

Stark broke into a hearty laugh.

"Jack, Ms. Benson is our public relations director for Universal Salvage, Incorporated. That's U.S. Inc. I thought it a classy choice of name."

"To U.S. Incorporated." Borodine raised his glass. They all followed.

Chapter Twelve

It was late in the evening when Carol and Boxer walked along the moonlit beach. The tide was ebbed and there was the slightest hint of a breeze on the Virginia shore. Boxer reminded himself that Stark sure knew how to pick a place to retire to . . . or at least to run a corporation from.

"You know, everything has been so crazy in the last month or two. I didn't have a chance to thank you . . . not properly, anyway. You waged a one-woman war with the media and the Navy. It has to have had an impact on the court-martial board." He took her hand in his as they walked. It was warm and her grip was firm.

"You know, Jack," she said looking up at him in that special way women have when they want to be kissed. ". . . I might have had ulterior motives."

He grinned down at her. "Why, Miss Benson, do you mean to tell me that your motives were not simply to prevent a gross miscarriage of justice?"

"Well, that . . . too," she said coyly.

"And . . ." Boxer warmed to the game. He knew

how it would end. ". . . you mean that you did *not* do what you did to become a shining light of journalistic excellence and win a Pulitzer?"

"Yes, Jack. There are already side benefits."

"And . . ." He forced himself to suppress a laugh. "What are the other side benefits?"

This time she could hardly manage to hide a giggle.

"Well, there is the moonlight and the ocean and . . ." She stopped and looked up at him, as she swept a reddish hair from her forehead. ". . . other things."

Boxer took her in his arms and kissed her. She sighed. Both of them had grown tired of games.

After a long time, she pulled away. "I can't breathe," she said.

He looked at the distance between them and the house. "Back to the house?" he whispered.

"Here," she intoned, her voice throaty and dry.

She unfolded the thin blanket she had been carrying with them and spread it in one, expert movement upon the sand.

They moved down to the blanket and Boxer slid a hand to her knee moving it slowly, but inexorably upward. She wore no pantyhose and when his hand arrived at its destination, he found she also wore no underwear. He was finding himself the *seduced* and not the seducer. He could not remember many times that had happened in his life.

"Hurry, Jack," she whispered.

Her pubic hair was soft but sticky wet.

154

Yes . . . hurry, he thought. There would be time for all of the luscious preliminaries the next time.

He snapped open his belt and unzipped, moving his slacks down to his knees. He entered her in seconds and thrust upward hard. She groaned through her teeth.

Only a matter of minutes later they lay together in a tangle . . . clothes hopelessly jumbled. The stars were barely visible through a slight haze. Boxer could make out Scorpio which had replaced its winter cousin, Orion. Her head was on his chest and his hand was tangled in her incredible silky, auburn hair.

"Did I mention I had been in the brig a long time?" he asked.

She started to laugh. "No. Did I mention that I waited a long time for you to get out?"

They laughed together.

"I didn't know . . ." he started to say. She reached a hand up and covered his mouth.

"Don't say anything, Jack. Nothing has to be said . . . not now at least. It was wonderful and I don't have a regret in the world. Let's not wreck things with conversation."

"I. . . . What the hell?"

He happened to be looking back in the direction of Stark's house when all of the outside lights came on at once. The back of the house and deck overlooking the beach was lit like a Christmas tree.

He could see two figures run down the back stairs to the beach. As the two hit the beach they turned

155

in opposite directions and started trotting down the beach with flashlights in their hands.

There was no question where they were headed or who they were looking for.

"I think we're going to have company in a minute or two."

It only took them half the time to rearrange their clothes and get to their feet.

It turned out that the one running in their direction was Borodine.

He was winded when he got them in sight and called to them. He slowed to a walk and started to regain his breath. "I *am* getting a little old for this, Comrade Boxer."

"What is so all fired important that you have to get out here and interrupt our . . . walk?"

Borodine looked to Carol and then back to Boxer. Boxer could see the unspoken comment in the Russian's eyes.

Walk, huh? Is that what they're calling it now? Borodine's eyes exclaimed.

"There are three men back at the house. They claim they are from the National Security Agency. They have credentials that seem good and they are in a hell of a hurry to see you. Obviously, they did not say why. It was all the admiral could do from preventing them from searching the beach with their on-call helicopter. We thought it better to search ourselves. We said it would arouse less uproar from the neighbors. Fortunate, weren't we?" Borodine grinned.

"We certainly were," Carol said, with a larger grin. She and Boxer exchanged grateful glances, and Borodine tried not to break out laughing.

The three headed to the back porch and as they got to the steps, Borodine snapped his fingers.

"Oh, I almost forgot to mention that these men said you might remember them, Jack."

"Oh," Boxer said, suspiciously.

They got to the top of the stairs and Boxer saw the familiar faces Borodine had mentioned. They were the same men who had met him in the exercise yard at the Norfolk prison.

Boxer was tempted to walk up to the taller of the two men and pop him one on general principles. But, his self-discipline took over and he resisted the temptation.

"Admiral Boxer, you might remember that my name is Riggs and these gentlemen are Quarterminn and Bradley. Ah, the gentleman who we represent is seeking another meeting with you. It is something of an emergency and he would like to speak to you about it."

Boxer had to think elliptically for a long minute before he responded.

"Tell the gentleman that I am engaged in working for a professional corporation called Universal Salvage, Inc. and if he wishes to retain me, he will have to retain my company."

Riggs looked at both Quarterminn and Bradley.

"Sir, we don't have the authority to assure that right here. We could either get on the phone and get

157

authority or assure you that it can be looked into later?"

"Get the authority now, gentlemen. U.S. Inc. consultation fees for a . . . corporation of your size will start with a million dollar retainer."

Borodine, Stark, and Carol looked back and forth between Boxer and Riggs. All three of them were confused but seemed to have confidence in Boxer to pull off whatever he was doing.

The three men retreated to their long, black limo in the driveway and Borodine looked to Boxer.

"Excuse me, but what the hell was all that about? Are we charging someone a million dollar consultation fee? If so, is there a chance that I can know who it is?"

"Yes, we are, Igor. We'll see in a minute if they are willing to pay or not. If they are, then the million is just for openers. But, I have a feeling we will have to be prepared to move with some speed."

He was right, as things turned out.

It was only five or so minutes when the trio of government men returned from their car.

Riggs spoke. His face was red and it was certain he had been chewed out by someone on the phone. Boxer could not be sure. After all, Riggs was not responsible for the payment of a million dollar retainer.

"We have an agreement, Admiral. The . . . organization I represent will contact your firm tomorrow and make the arrangements."

"Good." Boxer smiled broadly. He had brought the

office of the President of the United States to his terms. Whatever they needed him for, it had to be big for them to pay such a large retainer.

"There is one problem, sir. This is a delicate matter, and I believe this woman is Ms. Carol Benson who is affiliated with a number of newspaper chains and had been in the employ of a television network news operation? Is that correct, ma'am?"

"Yes, it is," Carol responded. "I don't remember being called ma'am in years. That alone was worth the trip."

Riggs was solicitous. "The problem is ma'am . . ." he smiled broadly. "Some habits are hard to lose. Excuse me. The problem is one just now of security. I have to speak to these men about issues for which their company has been retained. As an outside entity, and a newswoman, you do not have a need to know this material. I'm sure you understand."

"I certainly do understand, Mister Riggs. But, I am the newest member of the company. Admiral Stark and the rest of the board members . . ." her gesture expanded to indicate Boxer and Borodine, ". . . have approved the appointment. All of this was carried out this afternoon. Though, some of the concluding appointment activities were not culminated until tonight." Her eyes darted to Boxer who covered his mouth with his hand.

Riggs and the others looked confused but they managed to press on.

Riggs took the lead. "If you are a member of the organization, then we will include you in the National Security document that we are going to ask the others to sign. When you sign it you are officially governed by the National Security Act and under no conditions can you act in the role of a journalist."

"I think I understand," she said.

"The penalty for a breach of this security is a fifty thousand dollar fine and twenty years in a federal prison."

"I think I understand that, too, Mister Riggs."

When the agreements were signed and witnessed, Riggs seemed to relax as did his colleagues.

"We are going to have to ask for a meeting between our superior and Admiral Boxer alone. We have been ordered to return here tomorrow . . . actually . . . later this morning to escort the admiral to the meeting. We assume that the admiral is empowered by the corporation to negotiate further terms and make corporate commitments?"

Boxer looked to the other three and then he turned to Riggs.

"You assume correctly."

"We will return at 7:00 A.M. Please be prepared for a helicopter flight, Admiral."

"Very well," Boxer said.

In a minute, the three were gone.

"Will someone tell me what that was all about?" Borodine asked. "I, a Russian national, sign one of your security agreements. She, a world known journalist, does the same. Boxer, they must want *you* a great deal."

160

"I think they started wanting me but had to buy into the whole show in order to get me. It doesn't matter, there is a chance that the whole operation will not have a great deal to do with salvage.

"What had you seen as a time line to get a *Seawolf* class boat and have her refitted?" Boxer asked Stark.

"Something over a year, Jack. Remember, I wanted to have Sherwood Forest removed and replaced with deep rescue gear."

"Excuse me?" Carol interrupted. "I thought Sherwood Forest was in England near Nottingham?"

Boxer laughed. "It is. The real one is, that is. Boomers, nuclear subs, that carry ICBMs carry them in an area called Sherwood Forest because the tubes resemble the trunks of trees. The nickname goes back to the *Polaris* subs decades ago."

"We have something similar in our *Typhoon* class boats. Only difference is that our boats have the launching area in the bow and you have them aft of the sail," Borodine added.

"Well, I don't think we are going to have that year to fit out something. Whatever we are going to have to do on this deal, we will have to travel shanks mare."

It was Stark who suggested that they all turn in. It was a foregone conclusion that Carol was being offered a guest room, one of the fifteen or so that the admiral had available.

Stark and Borodine headed off to bed, leaving Boxer and Carol in the living room.

She looked across at him and started to chuckle.

161

"Is this what getting involved with you means? I know you are a man of action. The maneuvers on the beach tell me I like you, Admiral. But, cloak and dagger . . . so fast? It's almost as if you cranked those guys up to interrupt our little beach . . . encounter."

Boxer shook his head ironically. "Believe me, there is nothing I wouldn't give to have passed that interruption up. I was having too good a time."

He crossed the three feet that separated them and took her in his arms. They kissed and he found her lips were cool against his. Her mood had changed.

She pushed away after a second. "We both have to get some sleep. You have some sort of strange rendezvous in the morning and we can only guess where . . . with whom and what about."

That was it, he thought. Her reporter's curiosity. She was already regretting signing the agreement which had been one of the most iron-clad security agreements that Boxer had ever seen . . . bar none. He tried to turn things around. If he had been the journalist and she had been the admiral, how would he react? Was there a chance that he might be pissed about the secrecy?

Yes, he thought. There was a chance that he would feel left out as she did.

"I promise that I will tell you before anyone else. I mean . . . as soon as possible without getting myself put back in one of those Norfolk cells. Will that make things a little better?"

"Well, perhaps a bit," she said.

He could see that she had not expected to hear his words. They pleased her.

He took a step closer.

She backed away.

"We have to get some sleep. You especially. You have your big top secret meeting in the morning, right?"

He grabbed her and swept her into his arms.

"To hell with rest. I'll rest after the meeting."

She curled her arms around his neck as he started to negotiate the stairs.

"So will I," she cooed.

Chapter Thirteen

The helicopter came precisely at 7:00 A.M. As Boxer expected, it was one of the Marine Corps mini Chinooks with a glistening paint job and all of the spit and polish expected of such an aircraft. She landed as quietly as any helicopter could in a location that was not accustomed to them.

Boxer, in a business suit in which he was not totally comfortable, came from the back of the house, across the deck and walked up the steps into the helicopter. A Marine guard ushered him into a seat and the Chinook was off and airborne in a matter of seconds.

The flight took under a half hour and Boxer wasn't sure of the direction since he was not near a window. When the craft set down and Boxer stepped from the hatch he was in a sylvan setting that he thought might be in the Maryland mountains. It took him only a minute to figure out that his guess was right. He was at Camp David.

The President met him at the back door of the "summer cabin" as it was called. Eisenhower had spent a lot of time here, and it was the site where Carter had helped to forge the Camp David Accords between Begin and Sadat. Boxer felt in impressive company.

"Glad you could make it, Admiral."

"I'm afraid that title's gone, Mister President," Boxer said. There was more than a touch of sincere sorrow in his voice.

"It doesn't have to be gone forever, Mister Boxer. But, more about that, later. I am informed that we are under a tentative contractual agreement with your firm and that all of your people have been signed to a security agreement. Is that correct?"

"Yes, Mister President."

"Good, then I can speak freely. Please come inside."

They moved into the cabin's formal meeting room. It was done in rustic knotty pine and a window commanded a view of the mid-summer foliage of the Maryland Mountains.

The President directed Boxer to a seat while he leaned against the side of his small work desk.

"Jack, how much do you know about the Java strike?"

Boxer shrugged. "Supposed to be the biggest oil strike in the history of the planet. What I heard before all of the hot zone madness erupted was that there was a chance that the strike could alter the balance of oil power for perhaps a century. Sure would kick the shit out of the towel heads."

The President looked sternly at him. Boxer realized that his pejorative term for the Arabs did not sit well with the President, who moved from the side of the desk and paced in front of the picture window as he spoke.

"No matter how colorful your delivery, Jack, what you say is essentially true. No one had managed to find the limits of the Java strike yet. There is a chance that no one *ever will*."

"Excuse me, Mister President?"

"The reason that no one might ever plumb the depths of the Java strike, Jack, is that someone is destroying the rigs that have been put there. Needless to say, the companies that have invested in those destroyed rigs are not currently thinking about opening more drilling sites. They have already lost millions of dollars in investment not to mention hundreds of lives."

Boxer was incredulous. "Rigs are being destroyed? How? What method? How many? Where w—"

"Whoa . . . slow down. All in good time. Harry Olsen will be joining us in a few minutes and he will be able to give you a more complete briefing than I. What I can say is that we do not need an official American presence in this area. The Indonesian government would not appreciate that and OPEC would get a little twitchy if we were to send a task force. So . . ."

"So, enter U.S. Inc.?"

"Something like that."

"This sounds like a combat mission, Mister President. Truthfully, it is a bit premature for the operation we had been envisioning in U.S. Inc.'s scope."

"I assume you say that as you have not yet got a

submarine in the condition you want for the work you might be called upon to do?"

Boxer shook his head and waved a hand in surrender.

"Mister President, you seem to be a step ahead of me every way I turn. Can I ask some questions?"

"Certainly, though I will have to defer to Olsen on some of them, I'm sure."

"How many rigs were hit?"

"The count stands at seven, out of fourteen, now."

"The method?"

"Torpedoes, mostly. In one case the rig was pulled off the shelf and into the Java trench. She was never heard from again."

"Sir, are these torpedoes sub launched?"

"That's the current thinking. There was one man . . . an American in fact . . . picked up out of the water. It seems that he was the only survivor recovered so far from the *Exxon-Indonesia*. He reports that their sonar signals were identifying a class of Soviet sub called an *Alfa*. This sub destroyed their minis, their underwater drilling rig and the mother ship where the captain was the only survivor. There were well over a hundred men dead and damage in the hundreds of millions . . . not to mention that there is a blowout fracture in one of the drill holes . . . I think it's the Royal Dutch Shell operation. We have millions of gallons of oil, pouring out of that one every day."

The President was in full pace now. The man was angry, concerned . . . perhaps even frightened.

"What's the price per gallon running now on

light, sweet crude, Mister President?"

The President shook his head and closed his eyes with a sarcastic smile. "It's been bouncing up and down a lot. Just now, it's in the fifty a barrel range. It can't hold there for long."

"I guess not. I assume you think that this was done by . . . shall I say . . . OPEC operatives?"

"I don't know. I have assurances from every Arab power . . . all of the emirates . . . the Saudis. They are ready to swear on their grandmothers' graves that they are not doing anything in the strike."

"Do you believe them?"

"There is more than the short-term price of oil at stake here . . . at least for the Arabs. They have to worry about their financial position in the rest of the world. They have debts and interlocking trade agreements that can wreak havoc with the rest of their economies if other world powers gang up on them."

"Well, if the Arabs are out as suspects, there are always terrorists."

"I'll leave that for Olsen to speak about. Simply put, he doesn't think they are involved . . . not the classical groups at any rate."

They were interrupted by the arrival of the CIA director who brought bad news.

"Another one?" the President snapped.

"Yes, Mister President. It was a mother ship. This one was from British Petroleum. She was hit by a fish and sunk some three hours ago. We are still evaluating information on it. But, it looks like there has been considerable loss of life. None of the crew had a chance to get off."

"Was she connected to a seafloor rig?" Boxer asked.

"No . . . luckily," Olsen replied. "The rig she was to be connected to was still en route. If they had waited a week or two longer, they could have had both the rig and the mother ship."

"Mister Olsen," Boxer asked hesitantly. "Are there environmental groups that would be so radical as to . . . ?"

Olsen shook his head. "Not that we know of, Admiral. I shudder at the thought that there might be such groups out there somewhere, though. But if there were and they were carrying out this destruction, there would have to have been something like a demand. There has been no demand. And, oil is gushing into the strike creating additional environmental damage that we cannot yet even measure. No, we have to look in another quarter. And, my people say it must be among those who have heavy investments in OPEC right now . . . rather than members of the Arab oil community or any of the others we've mentioned."

"Have you managed to narrow the field, Harry?" the President asked.

"Yes, Mister President. We have several conglomerates. One of them came up on two computer searches. Surprising really. The first search involved the hot zone case."

"What?" Boxer exclaimed.

"You heard right, Admiral," Olsen said. "There is a chance that there is a connection. Not a great chance, of course. But a possibility."

"I know the admiral has vested interest in who might have spurred his actions but I have to be concerned with this crisis just now. What is the best bet, Harry?"

"It's only an educated guess, Mister President. But, my staff seems to think that the best bet for the entity that would make the most short-term profit from the destruction in the strike area is a Zurich-based operation called World Wide Disposal Corporation. They have acquired the largest blocks of OPEC stock and North Sea futures along with US Gulf licenses in the last six months. The prices they bought at have been pushed up two and three hundred percent. We have asked the SEC and the EEC's stock watch operation to see if they are preparing a large sell just about now. If they sell off a large amount in the next three days or so, they are our best bet for the ones who are at least financing the culprits.

"Mister President, there is also a rumor in the nautical community that there had been a sub deal with the Russian Navy. They have already sold a number of their frigates to foreign interests. We have been closely watching a sale they made to Libya and another to North Korea. But, the most important sale is one that we cannot document," Olsen stopped and looked through his paper.

"Yes . . . here it is. The Russian Navy is short three submarines. Their count is off by those three from the inventory that was taken eight months ago."

Boxer raised a hand. "Are we sure the count is

right? Is there a chance that this is a paper mistake?"

"There is always that chance," Olsen responded. "But the odds are small, and there is a better chance that there has been a covert sale. They would want to keep that secret."

"What kind of subs?" Boxer asked.

"As far as we can tell, they are *Alfas* . . . attack submarines . . . quite capable of carrying out the torpedo attacks mentioned in the reports."

The President turned to Boxer. "What's the operating depth for the *Alfa*, Jack?"

"They can maneuver and operate at twelve hundred feet, Mister President."

"They could be capable of coming *up* from the trench . . . carrying out an attack and then hiding back in the trench?" the President asked.

"Harry, if we destroyed these subs then the company who had driven up the price of oil would sell their holdings very quickly. Would you agree?" Boxer was fired up.

"Absolutely, sir."

"The solution then seems simple . . . relatively speaking. I get out there and sink one or more subs. You said there were three sold by the Russians, Mister Director?"

"Yes," Olsen answered.

"Well, I would need a considerable sub to take on three *Alfas*. But, I think I could do it."

The President turned to Boxer. "You will have a *Seawolf*, Jack. We had to discontinue production but we have three prototypes available. One of them is

171

fitted out for anti-sub combat. Just on loan . . . I'm afraid. But, it's yours."

The President looked from the picture window and then he turned back to Olsen.

"I gather we can deal with the organization that is behind this destruction when the admiral, I have every confidence, destroys these recently sold *Alfas*."

"I am sure that if the admiral can take out the *Alfas*, there is a good chance that we can follow through with the company."

Boxer got to his feet. "It sounds like I should be getting on my way. I expect I will have to maneuver a sub halfway around the world to get to the Java strike."

"Not at all, Admiral," the President said. "We moved the SSN-SW1 into the Philippines a week ago. You simply have to pick your crew and get aboard. There will be training personnel aboard waiting for you. You will need a crash course, though the SSN-SW1, I am told, is not that different from the SSN-S1 that you appropriated for your run to the North Pacific. The helicopter's waiting, Admiral. Better get going."

"Yes, sir."

Boxer strode from the office and felt the pride of command and the excitement of a challenge stirring within. No one had taken on more than one *Alfa* before to his knowledge. Then again, no *Seawolf* class boat had ever gone into combat, at least not as far as he remembered. He headed to the helicopter and juggled a dozen mental alternatives as he swung into his seat.

* * *

The President and Harry Olsen watched as the helicopter took off in swirling dust into the summer sky. They watched as it banked and turned south in the direction of the Virginia shore.

"Well, Mister President, do you think Boxer can stop three subs?"

The President looked at the small dot that the helicopter had become.

"If there is anyone who can, Harry, it's him. It's Boxer."

Chapter Fourteen

Eric looked at the oil reserves map of the world on the computer screen. Each map had a floating price that was keyed to the most current prices on the world markets. The price per barrel was hovering at fifty-five dollars. He wondered how long they could remain in that range before the world governments stepped in and started taking over oil producing countries. The problem was a delicate one. He had to keep the price as high as he could for as long as he could without de-stabilizing the oil producing governments. Then, he would step into two of the emirates where he had large, hidden holdings and topple the emirs with coups. After the deposed emirs were replaced with *his* men, he would radically drop the price of oil and de-molish the rest of the market. There was little question that, as long as no one ever went back into the Java strike, he would have virtual control of the world's oil supply for decades.

As he saw it, the world did not need more oil . . . it simply needed centralized control of it. And, that centralization would allow him to recoup the losses suffered in the hot zone episode.

It was the thought of the hot zone that reminded him of Boxer. Had he been a man prone to rage, he would have gotten angry over the thought of the American adventurer. But, Eric Von was not a man who was prone to getting angry. He had not risen to the position he held by losing his temper. He only took radical action against individuals when the situation required.

It was starting to look, however, like action in the Boxer affair was required . . . again. The first attempt had failed. But, that had been a calculated risk all along. The one member of the court-martial board who Eric's operatives had bought did not succeed in getting the good admiral behind bars and out of the way. That was simply the way the dice fell. Admiral Walford had been too formidable a nut to crack for Eric's operative. Spilt milk.

But, the numbers Eric was seeing on his monitors were too great for any one man or small group of men to contravene. That was why he had ordered constant updates on Boxer.

He pressed his intercom switch.

"Send the gentleman in, please," he said.

While there was no verbal response to his order, the door to his office opened immediately.

Nguyan Lo was tall for a Vietnamese. He had been a part of the team that had planned the 1968 Tet US Embassy raid for General Giap. He had left the control of the party when money overcame political ambition and he had ultimately become a mercenary with a specialization in tapping into enemy computer systems. He had discovered that playing with computers was much more interesting than getting shot at and napalmed.

"Have a seat, please, Lo."

Dutifully, the Vietnamese sat in the large padded chair.

"What have you got on Boxer, Lo?"

Lo had a notepad open in front of him but Von Stempler noticed that the man's eyes never went to it. He liked that.

"At midnight GMT . . . that would be 2:00 A.M. Central European Time, my team executed a 'slurp' on the data feed between JCS and field commands. The feed was encrypted but it was nothing we couldn't break easily. It only took the CRAY de-crypt random access program about an hour to do the cypher—"

"I know you are the best at this sort of thing. Get to the specifics."

"It seems that the American Department of the Navy has activated an accounting code that allows for Black Budget transfer of the SSN-SW1 to another category."

"One of the *Seawolf* class?"

"Yes, sir. The transfer went off in a routine manner. However, the fact that the classification was TS-COSMIC and the fact that the transfer was Black Budget in the first place says it was something important. My people created another 'slurp' at the receiving end of the transmission and came up with some interesting results."

He paused finally to look at his notes. His "slurp" had been an intercept of telemetry data fed through satellite. All one needed was a dish above the horizon to intercept such information and a fortune in sophisticated computer and encryption hardware to carry out what Lo's team had done. But, one also needed the creativity and the daring. All of these were things Lo had in enormous quantity.

Von Stempler nodded.

"Well, we checked the receiving end and found that there was a receipt of signal message sent in the clear . . . no encryption."

"Isn't that unusual?"

"Damned unusual for government traffic."

"And — ?"

"We assumed that there would be a sign-off of sorts when the signal was completed. The sign-off was also in the clear and the codes in the sign-off were traceable through various United States state sub-nets. The Americans have never had good security on them.

"As it turns out, the receiving party was an American firm called U.S. Incorporated."

"A standard American government contractor?" Von Stempler asked.

"No. Or, not until recently," Lo responded.

"Meaning?"

"The organization, a marine salvage corporation called U.S. Incorporated, has only been on the books for a month. It is odd that it would have gotten a government contract so fast. It's miraculous, in fact."

"How does this tie together with what I was looking for . . . Boxer and his people?"

Lo smiled thinly. He looked down at his notes a second time. He was warming to the task.

"The incorporation papers were in the Commonwealth of Virginia and it has its operation on computer . . . connected to the state system. It was not hard to tie into their records and enter the corporate licensing database. We found that the principal officer of the corporation was a man named Stark . . . retired Vice Admiral Thomas Stark."

"Boxer's former superior?"

"Yes, sir. And the other officers were a man named Igor Borodine and Admiral Jack Boxer. There was a fourth member . . . a woman named . . ." He consulted his notes. "Ah . . . Carol Benson. She is listed as public relations director. She was instrumental in getting a great deal of favorable publicity for Admiral Boxer during his court-martial."

"Boxer's whore," Von Stempler intoned.

"I have no information on that, sir," the Vietnamese grinned.

Von Stempler nodded. "Go on."

"I think it safe to conclude that the transfer from the JCS and US Navy was a *Seawolf* class boat to this corporation . . . and Admiral Boxer."

"And," Eric mused, "how many places could they be sending the *Seawolf* boat?"

"I have information on that . . . at least grounds for good speculation. We have another intercept. This one is a part of our normal monitoring system . . . not a 'slurp.' It was sent to CINCPAC in Hawaii. The text was encrypted but, as before, yielded easily to coaxing. The text was a warning that an American *SW* class boat would be crossing the Pacific submerged in a stealth mode. It was sent as a guideline and warning to American patrol boats, especially *Trident* class, Boomers, as they are called and *Los Angeles* class attack boats on patrol and also submerged in the area. The

178

identifying *Seawolf* sonar signature would be enough to warn them away."

"They want free reign for the *SW* to cross the Pacific."

"Yes. And the commands indicate that she will be heading in the direction of the Philippines."

"A staging area? A training ground?"

"Perhaps both, sir. The Java strike is easily within the cruise radius of a *Seawolf* class boat and there is a good chance he could be searching for something there."

Eric reminded himself that Lo knew nothing of *Krieg,* or at least, Eric thought the man knew nothing. When it came to Lo, there were always things that you could not approach with absolute certainty. The man was slippery. Nevertheless, there was no question that Boxer who had eluded Eric Von several times now was headed to the Java strike with the aim of stopping the interdiction. That could not be allowed to happen.

"Has your staff carried out the communications security precautions I asked for?"

"Yes, sir. The COMMO link is close to impossible to break or intercept."

"Close to?"

"Yes, sir. There is no such thing as an unbreakable system. Look at what we have been doing to the United States' systems. Everything we have acquired is classified. Everything has gone through multiple systems checks. Suffice it to say that this system is close to impossible to break. It will, however, only remain that way for a matter of a week or ten days."

"Why?" Eric Von Stempler asked indignantly.

"To attract the attention of the security and intelligence community is something that will eventually challenge people. Eventually, they will break the system. Use it for your purposes. When you need another, I will devise one. I already am devising one, in fact."

"That's good, Lo. You can go."

"Very well, sir," the Vietnamese said before he turned on his heel and left.

Von Stempler reminded himself that he should give Nguyan Lo a large bonus. If not for the work done then for the fact that he wanted to keep such a man as an ally rather than an enemy.

He moved to the wall opposite the picture window and pressed a stud. The room darkened as the two panes of polarized glass rotated against one another preventing sunlight from entering. It would keep out prying telescopes and binoculars.

He moved a series of slides on a coded panel and part of the wall slid away to reveal a communications center.

The audio pickup was very sensitive. There was no volume to be set. All Von Stempler had to do was check his watch to see that his commanders were on station.

"Good morning, gentlemen," he said. "Or, good day, as it is not morning where you are."

At three locations in the Java Sea, three *Alfa* subs, armed and eager to hunt, transmitted a response.

"*Krieg* One, you are in command of the operation." Von Stempler briefed Captain Helmut Schlag, late of the *Kriegsmarine,* on the conversation he had been having with Lo. *Krieg* Two commander Han T'Sung, late of the PRC Navy, and *Krieg* Skipper Vladimir

Kalienko, formerly of the Red Navy, listened in.

There was a slight delay before the answer was transmitted. Eric Von was certain that this had something to do with the incredible encrypting procedure that totally laundered the communication in both directions.

"It would seem, sir, that he would move south through the Celebes Sea. He could hug the Borneo Coast through the Straits of Makassar and once he turned the point at Banjarmasin he'd be in open, deep water. An *SW* class boat could be dangerous against any of our *Typhoon* class. I suggest we spread across the straits and wait for him there."

Again, there was a pause. "And, if he comes the long way . . . through the South China Sea and comes down the west Borneo coast. Would he not then be in deep water and behind you?"

There was a blast of static and the voice that responded was Oriental. It was T'Sung. "Perhaps two boats in the straits and one on the west Borneo coast?"

"Bad tactics!" It was the gruff voice of Kalienko. "You split your force and he can take you piecemeal. There is a chance with two *Alfas* against a single *SW* class. Alone, any one is vulnerable. Three teamed give us a considerable edge. Never split the force. Remember the American Custer? He split his force. What happened to him?"

There was another pause and another blast of static and Von Stempler spoke to the three of them.

"Devise the best plan you can. I personally lean toward the strength in numbers approach. Find him, triangulate him, then destroy him. But, you are the experts. I will pay a half million American dollars to the boat that first confirms that his fish killed Boxer's boat. I leave the rest to you."

Von Stempler flipped a switch that both disengaged the radio and started the wall panel skidding back into position. The morning sun was lighting the northern-most region of the Alps across the Zurichsee. The view was magnificent.

Chapter Fifteen

Boxer and Sarkis came aboard at a small cove, rented at an exorbitant fee from the Philippines government. Manila had simply looked the other way when the US Navy Seabees, disguised as civilian construction workers, built the DeLong Pier in the deep water coral lagoon. She sported a ninety-foot depth at low tide with a three-foot tidal shift range which allowed the construction teams to work with a great deal of speed.

They entered the sail and climbed down to the control room, spending time greeting old comrades on the way. It didn't take Boxer, Sarkis, and Borodine long to see that the new *SW* class was incredible. While the old *Trident* boats required a crew of seventy to eighty, automation had reduced this number drastically on the *SW* class. Twenty men and three or four officers could run all of her operations with ease.

A great deal of her routine operations were identical to those of the SSN-S1, and the specialized ones that remained had been crash-learned by Sarkis, Borodine, and Boxer in a matter of days. Still, they didn't have the "feel" of the boat and there would be no time to get it. They were going to have to get to sea and head to the Java strike immediately. The shakedown cruise would also be a war patrol.

So what's different, Boxer thought. Everything is as it was except that he was now a civilian and not in the Navy. While there was a bit of sorrow, a modicum of bitterness and more than a touch of anger left in him, he quickly realized that he was making more than ten times what he had been making in the Navy. He was simply being a mercenary for the same boss.

So what's different?

"I have the conn," Boxer said standing in the middle of the control room.

"Prepare to get under way," he said in a command voice that he was happy to be able to use again.

"Standby to cast off bow and stern lines," Sarkis ordered.

"Cast off all lines," Boxer called.

"Lines are off, sir," Sarkis reported.

Boxer nodded. "Very well."

"Incoming tide is moving us into the stream," Sarkis said.

"Slow astern," Boxer said.

Sarkis dialed the order in the bridge MCC.

The SSN-S1's propeller began to turn, and the boat slowly moved backwards into the channel.

"Come to two seven five," Boxer said.

"Two seven five, aye," Sarkis repeated, moving the necessary control dial.

The stern of the boat began to bear toward the starboard, as it backed out into the channel.

"Tug is beginning to swing toward the pier," Sarkis reported.

"Give me a distance check to the pier," Boxer ordered.

Sarkis checked the radar display. "Five hundred yards."

"Stop all engines," Boxer ordered.

"Stop all engines," Sarkis repeated.

The *SW* sub continued to move backward, then slowed, and came to a full stop.

"Tug moving off," Boxer said. "Ahead, one third."

Sarkis repeated the command, and dialed in the speed.

"Come to new course two five nine," Boxer said.

"New course two five nine," Sarkis said, making the necessary adjustments.

They had cleared the channel and were in the open sea for close to an hour before Boxer came through the open hatchway onto the sail. Sarkis remained below, though Borodine joined Boxer.

"So," the Russian said. "We are here. And we are starting to know what to do with this magnificent piece of machinery. What we don't have is —"

"A plan?" Boxer interrupted.

"Exactly. You have ideas?"

"Yes and no. The first thing is to get to the Java Sea as soon as possible. The second is what I'm trying to figure out now. There is a good chance we are

185

facing more than one sub. Three is most likely. So, where would they be . . . who is running them and what do they know?"

"I think there is a chance that they know a great deal, my friend. Anyone who could buy three subs with *Alfas* running close to half a billion dollars apiece and then get the crew to run them must have a great deal of capital. More than the wealth of some countries, I think. Such a person would also have an exceptional intelligence system. They probably know that we have this sub and that we are getting under way. Whoever it —"

"Small object in the water," the lone lookout in the stern of the sail called.

"Bearing?" Boxer asked.

"Port beam . . . about three hundred yards out. She's low to the water. Looks like a dish or something . . . perhaps a buoy?"

Both Boxer and Borodine swung their glasses to the left and looked outward from the hull.

"Son of a bitch," Boxer snapped. "It's a fucking sonobuoy."

He reached down and stabbed at the intercom.

"Come right to course three four five. Clear the bridge . . . Dive the boat!"

The lookout scampered below as did Borodine. Boxer would be the last man down from the sail. He watched as the bow planes rigged out and caught the water driving the bow down where the positive buoyancy would be driven from the tanks by seawater. She was faster at a dive than any boat he had ever seen, even the SSN-S1. Water was planing across the

186

base of the sail as Boxer started to scamper down the ladder.

He swung the large hatch shut and spun the dogs into place.

"Hatch secure," he bellowed as he headed to the CR.

"I have the Conn," he yelled to Sarkis.

"Aye, aye, sir," Sarkis responded reflexively.

"Take her to periscope depth," Boxer ordered.

Sarkis responded and the boat levelled at seventy-nine feet. The keel depth was quite deep because of the height of the sail on this new generation of subs.

"Reading periscope depth, Captain," Billingsly, the chief of the boat, called from a few feet away.

"Very well," Boxer responded. "Sonar, what do you make of that thing?"

"Small-ranging transmitter, sir. Signal analysis indicates she is transmitting above the surface while she is probing on and under the surface."

"Sure as hell *is* a sonobuoy. Who the hell . . . ? Igor . . . the guys with the money, right?"

"I doubt if it belongs to our people, Jack. They know where we are."

"Well no matter who put it there, it is reporting our position right now. Perhaps there is a chance that we can convince them we're a school of fish. Take her to a hundred feet and give me a chaff release."

"Aye," Sarkis said and passed the order on.

Obediently the sub moved downward. As she levelled at a hundred feet, five hundred pounds of porous but lead foil mixed paper was released and floated like a cloud over the position that the *SW* boat had occupied.

"Chaff dispersing, sir," sonar reported.

"Sarkis?"

"Sir?"

"Get me every know this thing can give and head us out under cover of that chaff. Give me a heading of three six zero."

"Jack?" It was Borodine, frowning.

"What?"

"If we turn those knows we will be cavitating and they will hear us."

"I know there is a chance of that, Igor. But, there is also a chance they have reported our position already. If they have not reported us and have not resolved our signal as *Seawolf* class boat, we're clean."

Boxer moved through the red light that bathed the CR to the sonar operator and on to the UWIS console. He slipped into his seat.

"Have we got any active sonar?"

"Not now," sonar reported. "But, when we make thirty. . . ." The sarcasm of the remark was not lost on Boxer.

"Thirty-five knots," the helm reported.

"Distance to the sonobuoy?"

"Four miles," Sarkis reported.

"What's the effective range on an old Soviet sonobuoy, Igor?"

The Russian folded his arms.

"Eight to ten miles," Igor answered. "That's on an active signal."

"And on a passive?"

"About where we are now."

"That's what I thought. All stop. Rig for silent running."

Sarkis echoed the commands. All of the active machinery on the SW4 went silent and in a matter of seconds there was not a chance in the world that a detection system on earth could detect the *SW* boat. Her surface was laminar and she emitted a small cloud of bubbles at the nose of her teardrop shape. The water bubbles were designed to be swept back along the lines of the hull. They blurred the signal that a sonar operator either active or passive could get from her.

"Laminar flow steady, sir," Billingsly reported. "Silent running confirmed."

"What's our best possible speed at silent running?" Boxer asked Sarkis. Ordinarily he would know such details about the running of a boat he was skipper of, but they had precious little time on this boat, as incredible as she was. Boxer would have liked to have had more.

"Igor," Boxer called.

"Yes?"

"If you were the enemy, would you have posted one of those *Alfas* near the Philippines in the hopes that we would walk right into you, unsuspectingly . . . as you were so close to home?"

"Yes. It's taking the initiative. That's something most of us would do." He referred to the traditional aggressiveness and arrogance of sub drivers, no matter what their nationality. In many ways they were a great deal like tank commanders . . . audacity and speed were all that they had. Blessedly, though, sub drivers had a great deal more firepower than their tank conterparts.

"Sonar, remain passive but strain your ears. There is chance something's out there."

They did not have long to wait.

"Sonar contact," Billingsly yelled. "Bearing one-oh-eight relative. Range eighteen thousand yards. He's quiet, Skipper. Signal's almost not there."

Boxer came up from the captain's chair.

"Can we say type at this range?"

"We can try," Sarkis said, as he labored over the UWIS. After a minute he looked to Boxer. "It's an *Alfa*, Skipper."

"Go to battle stations," Boxer responded. "Also, get me as much information as you can on the UWIS."

Sarkis came on the 1MC. "Battle stations . . . All hands, battle stations."

"Target bearing changing to three zero relative. Range remains constant at twelve miles. Speed, zero six knots. Depth, three hundred ninety feet. And . . . she seems to be drifting with the current, Skipper," Sarkis reported.

The target was below them and generally off in the direction of their port bow. She was heading in a left to right direction.

"She's lying in the weeds, Igor. There's a chance she's waiting for us to take a northerly track. That would mean—"

"It would mean," the Russian interrupted, "that she expected us to head through the South China Sea and pass the west coast of Borneo."

190

"What would they consider our other options," Boxer asked, half to himself. "It would have to be south toward the Sulu Sea . . . the direct route.

"Well, Igor, do we bet that there is another one somewhere off to the south? So that if we avoid this one with his convenient sonobuoys, the one to the south would acquire us. The direct route." He looked to the Russian.

"Quite possible. That would mean a coordinated attack. And, perhaps one left behind to wrack havoc on the Java strike."

"Chief Billingsly, what armament have we got?"

"Six Mark XX wire guided homing fish. They're the best, Skipper. We have three more of them aft if we need them. We also have four Sea Darts and a full array of noisemakers and ECM. In that regard we're in great shape."

"New sonar contact," the sonarman's voice sent a chill through the CR staff.

"Bearing?" Boxer asked.

"One eight zero relative. Getting a read, now. She's going active with sonar. She'll be easy to read now."

"We have a complete UWIS reading," Sarkis called to Boxer who was listening to the distant sonar ping as it came back through fifteen thousand feet of seawater to their equipment.

Soviet Alfa *attack submarine nuclear powered . . . Maximum speed of surface twenty knots . . . Maximum speed submerged thirty-five knots . . . Armed with six standard torpedoes . . . Cruising range,*

191

"Figures," Boxer said. "Sarkis, code the one astern as *Costello* and the one ahead as *Abbott*. Read?"

"Aye, aye, sir."

"Where's current drift taking us?"

"In the direction of *Abbott*. She's still passive." It was Borodine who had taken the seat of the sonar man. Boxer was pleased. The Russian had a great deal of experience with sonar and many times plotted his own solution to firing problems by listening himself. It was also said that he was uncanny at figuring what the opposing skipper was going to do next.

Borodine cocked his head to the side. After a second, his eyes went to his scope.

"*Abbott* has gone active." The sonar for the *Alfa* ahead of them had started actively searching.

Boxer shook his head and slammed a palm down on his armrest. It had to have been when they went to flank. He had been wrong. It would be all that he could now do to save his boat. There was no secrecy . . . only a matter of time.

"Small transients!" the Russian yelled.

"Where away?" Boxer asked.

"From *Abbott*. We're pinpointed. I make it a spread of four torpedoes."

"Have they acquired?" Boxer asked.

"Negative, they are still seeking." The small sonar rigs in the noses of the torpedoes were searching actively for a target. The *Alfa* had started them off generally in the right direction but there was a

192

chance that they would home in on anything from whales to gravity slides.

"How much water beneath us?" Boxer asked.

"Two hundred feet. We're sliding off the side of the shelf. Estimate twelve minutes to twenty-five hundred feet of available depth," Sarkis volunteered. It was just the information that Boxer needed . . . not too much or too little. It was simply the way Sarkis was with Boxer. He knew what the old man needed.

"Hold the drift rate and stay on silent running, helm."

"Helm, aye," Billingsly responded.

"Where are these fish, Igor?"

"The spread is increasing and the range is nine thousand yards."

"Speed and direction?"

"Sixty knots and we are about in the center of the pattern."

"Very well."

Boxer could not hope that the cloud of bubbles created by the laminar passive defense system could help. The odds were very long that the SW was going to be able to comb through the torps that were closing on him. The small sonars were stupid and not very powerful but they were designed to work in sets such as these and they created a wall of active sonar signals in front of them and in all directions. The sonar could be deflected by very few things.

Suddenly Boxer thought of one of them.

"Sarkis, what have we got in heavyside? Where is the thermocline?"

"We have a thermocline . . . a thin one at about four-hundred-fifty feet. There is a thicker one at eleven hundred . . . but I don't think there is a way to get there unless we go active."

"It's a crapshoot. How much depth have we got?"

"Not enough," Igor answered. "We are sliding off but we only have four hundred. It will be another six minutes before we get enough depth to head for a thermocline."

Igor Borodine knew exactly what Boxer was thinking. He had pulled the same maneuver against the United States Navy as well as the NATO navies for years. If they managed to get below the thermocline there was a good chance that approaching torps as well as the active sonar of the attacking sub would be fooled by the layer of colder water. The torps would scurry in various directions until their fuel ran out and they started to sink.

"Sarkis, prepare noisemakers. A full spread."

"They're hot, Skipper. They were three minutes ago."

"Depth, Helm?"

Billingsly paused before he turned to Boxer.

"Seventy-seven feet, Skipper. We are starting to angle up. We need speed. The current is not enough."

Boxer had been afraid of that. Well, he thought, perhaps the time to go active was now. *Abbott* had gone active and *Costello* would join in a matter of minutes.

But, before he went active and allowed both subs to zero him, he would have to give them something

194

else to think about.

"Sarkis, get me a firing solution for *Abbott*. They are not the only ones who can spread a fan of torps."

"Take a second, Skipper."

"Understood. Distance to the torps?"

"Five thousand yards. One of them has acquired . . . now two. They are diverting from the others. Yes . . . yes . . ." Igor pressed the headset to his ears. "Two have us, for sure. Their course adjustments are too radical. Time to impact three minutes."

"Visual." Sarkis placed the UWIS screen in a symbolic mode. The sub coded *Abbott* was placed near the top of the screen. She was flashing red as she had fired her torpedoes. The torps themselves were dotted lines weaving their way in the direction of the *SW* which was in the center of the screen. The sub dubbed *Costello* remained blue and stood toward the south end of the screen. She was something that Boxer would have to deal with in minutes, or so he thought.

"Firing solution prepared, sir," Sarkis called out.

"Is the best solution a Sea Dart or torp?"

"Sea Dart, sir. Two of them are prepped."

"Very well. Depth and speed?"

It was Igor's turn. "Seven hundred feet, coming up to seventy . . . now sixty-eight. Bottom is dropping off at approximately three hundred feet a minute."

They had cleared the shelf and below them, the Sulu Deep was plummeting away from them. It was the best news Boxer could hear.

"All ahead flank. Blow remaining positive. Ten degrees down bubble. Crash dive one thousand feet. Fire both Sea Darts when ready. Everybody hang on to something."

A chorus of responses rang out. The *SW*'s huge bulk hunched forward as she built speed and ran seawater across her diving planes. In less than a minute the *SW* was roaring downward at an unbelievably steep angle. Crockery in her galley was sliding off shelves and tables as Boxer drove the sub down at an angle she was never meant to adopt.

"Where are those torps, Igor?"

"Two thousand yards for the two that are closing . . . the other two have run out of fuel . . . at least they are starting to sink. Ninety seconds to impact."

"Stand by with the noisemakers. Where are we with the Sea Darts, Sarkis?"

"Firing solution plotted. Prepared to fire."

"On my command. Launch . . . launch . . . launch."

"Sea Darts away." The *SW* bucked as the missiles were launched. A strange blend of missile and torpedo, they would break the surface and travel through the air like a rocket until they reached the coordinates of the target. Then, they would fall into the sea and start to act like a homing torpedo.

"Time to impact on the Sea Darts?"

Sarkis looked at the timing clock on his console.

"Two minutes thirty seconds," Sarkis answered.

"Time to impact on us?"

"Eighty-five seconds," Borodine reported. "The warheads have armed themselves. It seems that the computers think they have a good fix."

"Good," Boxer answered. Igor looked at him.

"I don't know that I feel that way, Jack."

"Tell ya why in a minute, Igor. Helm, what's the distance to the thermocline?"

"Seventy seconds to thermocline at this speed," Helm answered.

"Sarkis, be prepared to go to silent running the second we pass through."

"Aye, aye, sir," Sarkis answered.

The *SW* was rocketing downward in the direction of the layer of cold water where the temperature differential was some thirty degrees. The torps would, he could only hope, see this as a solid wall.

There was only a fifteen second differential between the sub passing through the thermocline and the torps reaching the sub.

"Engineering . . . can we get any more turns on the engines?"

"Negative," came a voice from over the intercom.

"We are at a hundred five percent now. She is not rated past a hundred. We might blow a coolant line or something and then we'd all get fried."

"Very well. Igor, give me the count. You, too, Sark. Have we got a hit probability on the Sea Darts?"

Billingsly had slipped into the gunnery officer's chair and was looking at the plot.

"Darts in the water in seven seconds. They will go active and head to the last position stated. Yes . . . there. They are in the water. *Abbott* is running a crash dive. She's headed for the thermocline, too."

"Thirty seconds to thermocline."

"Forty-five seconds to impact."

"Sarkis, stand by noisemakers."

"Aye, aye, sir," Sarkis replied. There was an edge to his voice. In all of the years he had known the man, Boxer did not remember hearing it before. Then again, they had never taken on an *Alfa* before . . . let alone two or three of them.

"What have we got on *Costello?*"

Borodine shook his head. "She went passive, Jack. She crawled back into the weeds."

"Times?"

"Fifteen to thermocline . . . twenty-five to impact," Igor replied after a second.

"Stand by noisemakers." Boxer counted in his head. "Release noisemakers . . . now . . . now . . . now."

On the rear hull of the *SW* astern of Sherwood Forest, the four ash can-sized containers were released from the hull. They immediately started to make electronic and mechanical noise that would sing in the ears of the torpedoes that they were the submarine the torps were seeking. The torp's computers were not normally sensitive to discriminate between the noisemakers and the sub.

"Entering thermocline," Borodine shouted.

Now comes the hard part, Boxer thought. They had to roar through the layer and hope that it closed sufficiently behind them so that the torps could "feel" nothing.

"Say when we're completely through."

Sarkis was already on it. "Three . . . two . . . one

198

. . . stern coming through . . . through thermocline."

"All stop! Silent running!" Boxer yelled.

There was no response. But, he could hear the power plant shutting down.

"Impact time to us?" he barely whispered.

"Eight sec—" Borodine was cut off in mid word. Two explosions went off within a split second of one another, not more than a hundred yards distant from one another. One of the following torps had hit the thermocline and had gone off; another of them had slammed into a noisemaker and activated its detonator setting off a ton of high explosives.

"Time to Sea Dart impact?" Boxer screamed to Borodine, who was pulling himself up off the deck and moving back into the sonar chair. He had forgotten to buckle the seatbelt.

"Seven seconds."

There was a sudden, screaming silence in the CR.

"Hit. We have a hit on Sea Dart one. There is a second detonation. Close aboard the first. Near miss."

"Can we confirm the hit?"

There was a pause and all eyes in the CR went to Borodine.

He did not answer for a long time.

It was a minute later when he pulled the headset off and turned to Boxer. "Sounds of pressure hull imploding Jack. *Abbott* is gone."

"Is there a position on *Costello?*"

The passive sonar array strained its electronic ears in an attempt to separate out normal sea noises from power plants, weapons systems and the general noise that a submarine made as it passed through the water.

Boxer pondered going to active sonar but he did not like the odds. His position was fairly clear or might become clear when he rose above the thermocline or started his engines. He decided to split the difference.

"Give me a single active ping, Igor. See if we can get anything."

"Very well."

Igor hit the active sonar button and the BONNNGGG of a single ping roared out from the *SW.*

Borodine hugged the headset.

"Nothing . . . Jack. She made a hole in the water and died there."

"No . . . dead she isn't, Igor. She isn't dead. She's very much alive . . . but where?"

Chapter Sixteen

Captain Vladimir Kalienko listened intently to the faint sounds in the headset. He nodded in resignation.

"The son of a bitch has destroyed Schlag and *Krieg* One. Almost certainly with a Sea Dart."

He turned to his Exec. "Yuri."

"Sir!"

"Rig for silent running. All stop. Check the drift. Will the current take us to him or not?"

Yuri, a small wiry man with a black moustache, was a study in contrast with his captain. Vladimir Kalienko was large and burly, fond of fat women and bar brawls. He seemed too big for the confines of the *Alfa*. Still, he knew when to stay quiet and let the enemy come to him.

The *Alfa* was a submarine designed to attack other submarines and it was supposed to have the advantage over the *Seawolf* class. Then again, Vlad reminded himself, no one really knew about the exact armament or performance characteristics of the *SW* boats. So few of them had ever been built; by the time they had been, the CIS had taken over for the Soviets and there was no longer a need for the *SW*.

What was it the American sub drivers called them? Boomers? Odd name, he thought. Gallows humor when the "boom" in question meant the end of the world.

A single *SW* class boat . . . an old *Trident* class boat, for that matter, could put three hundred to four hundred thermonuclear warheads on targeted cities and military bases in less then ten minutes from launch. So . . . the boom was considerable. Sub to sub, the *Alfa* was better. But, Captain Schlag had not been better. Boxer had been the better man in this first exchange. He had been more daring and resourceful. Vlad could listen to the battle on the sonar as if it was being related to him by a witness. Every sound was the betrayal of a tactic. Boxer's diving through that thermocline . . . which was where Vlad now hid his *Alfa* . . . was nothing less than a work of genius.

He had already analyzed the various command decisions that Helmut Schlag had carried out, and he was sure that the man's fatal errors fell into a fairly simple pattern. First, he positioned himself too deep to carry out an emergency blow if it was needed. There was a chance that decision cost the lives of the ship's crew. Second, he went active with his sonar too soon, allowing Boxer to come up with a counter plan. Third, he both fired his torpedoes too soon and underestimated the electronic accuracy of the Sea Dart A.S. missile.

Vladimir Kalienko would not make such mistakes.

"Captain . . . we have a six knot southbound current. Enough to hold depth at silent running but it takes us slightly away from the American. If he heads south, though, he heads right into us. If he heads northwest into the South China Sea, then he is out of sonar detection range in less than an hour."

"Very well."

So *how* do you think . . . Boxer? Kalienko challenged his foe mentally. Had you acquired me at any time? I am sure you must have. Then you have to know I am here, and you have to know my quandary. You do not have to find me as much as I have to find you. Kalienko grudgingly saluted his rival.

"Yes."

"Sir?" Yuri asked, confused for a moment.

"He will go straight for the Java strike. It is his mission. The American is a mission man and it will be of foremost importance to him."

Vladimir headed to the chart table. He pressed a button on the side of the chart console and got a look at a computer projection of his position and a twenty-mile sonar mock-up of his surroundings. The wreckage of the *Krieg* One was a shimmering series of red pixels on the console screen. There were a series of blue question marks where the *SW* was thought to be. None was close enough for any real firing solution to be developed.

After a few more seconds of thought, Vladimir had come up with a plan.

"Speed dead slow."

"Dead slow, aye," Yuri echoed.

"Come right to new course one eight zero. Let that current push us away from him."

"Right standard rudder . . . Helm answers. Coming on to one eight zero."

After a few moments, Yuri looked to his captain.

"Steady on one eight zero, Captain."

"Give me a small chaff release . . . nothing that would appear to be a new signal, Yuri. I need to have something to cover my getting up to speed."

"Aye, aye, sir."

The chaff was a slight trickle and in a few minutes with the prop wash to disperse it, it formed a small shroud of material impervious to sonar.

Vladimir calculated that he had a six to seven knot submerged speed edge over Boxer's *SW*. If Boxer went the South China Sea route, Vlad, in turn, could go at flank speed through the Sulu Sea, round Sudabeng Point on the Borneo southeast coast, and be on station half a day before the *SW* got there. With T'Sung and him both waiting, they would destroy the *SW* and split the half million bonus.

"Make turns for ahead one quarter. Hold course one eight zero."

"Aye, sir."

With utmost caution, Vladimir Kalienko waited an additional half hour before giving his next order.

"All ahead flank. Maintain course one eight zero."

Behind the chaff cloud, the enormous engines of the *Alfa* roared to life.

"Maintain silent running," Boxer ordered. He looked to the sonarman's station where Borodine hunched over his headset. "Igor, what do we have on that hit?"

The Russian shook his head. "Hull breaking up. Nothing more than that. She's in very deep water. There won't even be a radiation trace when her reactor goes. No buoys on the surface. She didn't have time to get one off. Too bad. They were brave men."

"I'm sorry, Admiral. I don't agree. They were cowards. We might have been the first real fight they were in. All they have been doing is murdering generally unarmed well rigs. I wouldn't glorify that. I wouldn't call it courage."

Borodine flushed for a second, but he realized that Boxer was right. Indeed, all these mercs were doing was murder. It was a brand of piracy that both men found heinous.

"You're right, Jack. I am sorry. I. . . ." He pulled his headset closer to his ears.

"What is it, Igor?"

The Russian held up a hand as he concentrated on what he was hearing.

He got up and went to the computer where he played back a small piece of sonar recorded tape. The sound was visually displayed on a screen that was barely visible to Boxer a few feet away. He could see little that was recognizable. But, it was the Russian who was the real expert.

"Igor . . . what?"

Borodine looked at the pattern. He played a second or two of the signal five or six times before he turned back to Boxer.

"I can't be sure what it is . . . not yet. It was very minute and very far off. I am going to wash it through the computer and see if when we reassemble it we come up with something. It would recommend that we stay at silent running and at battle stations."

"I have no intention of doing anything else," Boxer said with certitude.

Igor fed the information into the computer and waited while the machine's electronics estimated the signal from every possible angle. It took eight or nine minutes for the answer to come out. It was not very satisfactory: Subaquatic life migration.

"What the hell does that mean, Igor?"

"A school of fish. But, I don't believe it."

Igor keyed a series of commands into the computer: State mechanical equivalent.

There was a long pause while the analog side of the computer decided what it was trying to find and another way of expressing it to the humans who asked. Finally, it found the phrase for which it searched.

White noise.

"Yes!" Borodine jumped from the chair.

"What is it?" Boxer asked.

"White noise. You know, the stuff that allows you to filter out extraneous sounds and concentrate. It prevents eavesdropping."

"I know what white noise is. What does the computer mean when it uses it?"

The Russian grinned. "When the *SW* computers were programmed to identify sounds, according to this documentation," he pointed to a stack of technical manuals that had been pushed to the bulkhead in the last hectic minutes, "they considered evasion devices to be white underwater sound. That tiny bite of sound that we picked up on the passive was just that . . . white sound. It was the sound of chaff being released. But it seems it was released very slowly . . . perhaps to cover an escape."

"Where though?" Boxer asked.

Borodine looked through his hurriedly made notes

206

and his fingers flashed across the console keys.

"Bearing one eight zero. Range give or take some . . . about ten thousand yards. Ah, there's something else."

"What, Igor?"

"The range is opening. There is a slight negative doppler to the signal which is why the computer thought it was a school of fish . . . a 'subaquatic life migration.' "

"So, the other *Alfa* is hauling ass?"

"It would look that way."

Boxer shook his head.

Why wouldn't the *Alfa* captain stay where he was? He had to know that the Sulu Sea approach was the fastest to get me to the Java Sea. The position he was in would have been best. He could lie in the weeds and wait. He could kick the shit out of us if we came on him unaware.

"Not the way to play poker," Boxer snorted, coming out of his interior gymnastics.

Borodine smiled his eminently Russian smile.

"He is not playing poker. He is playing chess. He assumes he has assessed your plan of action properly and he is moving into a tactically sound position to receive it."

"There is something else he is doing when he moves into that position."

"What?" Borodine asked.

"He is setting a trap. His tactical position is too good here. He is gambling that he can get at least as good a one where he is headed. That's too big a gamble to take unless there is another factor."

"What would that be?" Borodine asked.

"He has help in the place where he is headed."

"Another sub . . . another . . . the third *Alfa?*"

"Right," Boxer chuckled. "He is trading his *good* position for what he thinks is an *unbeatable* one. The odds are worth the risk in his mind," Boxer concluded.

Boxer stretched and he turned to Sarkis.

"Come left to course one eight zero."

"Aye, sir," Sarkis responded.

"I want dead slow until we're out of detection range of that *Alfa*. Then, I want flank speed until we are at the edge of his listening range again. You follow the pattern, Sarkis?"

"I follow, sir. You want to leapfrog at the edge of his range so we can approach and close the last ten to fifteen thousand yards when we're ready. Right?"

"You have it. But, I want to do that in the Sulu Sea, while he's racing to a position where he thinks I'll turn up."

"We're gonna surprise the little shit, right?" Sarkis asked.

"Depends. What's the status of the Sea Darts?"

"One operational. There are three others available but they require fitting time and data update. I wouldn't count on them, Skipper."

"Torps?" Boxer asked, his brows furrowed.

"Six forward and four aft. Tubes loaded."

"Update the TDC each time we get the hint of a contact. And Igor?"

"Yes, Admiral?" the Russian said.

"Can you stay on the sonar? This guy is running for his buddy and I have to know where the buddy is."

"Very well, Admiral."

"Let's go chase this son of a bitch down," Boxer

snarled.

Some ten miles ahead of the *SW,* Vladimir Kalienko, running at periscope depth and flank speed on the *Alfa* called *Krieg* Two, dared to expose his position for long enough to inform *Krieg* Three of his plan.

On *Krieg* Three, Captain Han T'Sung considered his situation. If he stayed where he was, there was a chance that the American Boxer and his *Seawolf* sub would come to him. But, he thought, there was also a chance that the *SW* sub would not come. There was a chance that it would be trapped and killed by Kalienko somewhere in the Sulu Sea.

T'Sung paced the conning tower for several minutes before he started to query his chief engineer about flank speeds and his sonar man about their exposed profile at those speeds.

It was after another few minutes of consideration that he returned to the radio operator.

"Send encrypted to *Krieg* Two."

"Yes, sir?"

"We will join you at . . . send coordinates . . . in Sulu Sea."

"Aye, aye, sir."

T'Sung was not about to give away his half of the bonus money that Eric Von Stempler had promised.

On the *Seawolf,* Jack Boxer was heading into two *Alfas* rather than one. And . . . he didn't know it.

Chapter Seventeen

BONNNGGG!

"What the hell was that?" Sarkis yelled.

"I have the conn," Borodine called out in the CR. "Call Admiral Boxer from his quarters. Battle stations! Battle stations! What have you got, Sonar?" Borodine asked.

The sonarman hunched over his console.

"Active sonar ping . . . range twelve thousand yards. Bearing two seven zero, true."

"What?" Borodine asked with a combination of confusion and frustration.

"That's the correct range and heading, Admiral," Sarkis said from the other end of the CR. "I just verified it."

"What's the range and bearing to the original target?" Borodine asked.

"Fifteen thousand yards . . . bearing one eight zero," Sarkis responded.

"What the hell is that?" Borodine asked.

"Dollars to donuts it's the third *Alfa*," Boxer said as he came into the CR.

Sarkis moved to the UWIS. "Checking," he said. "Correct, sir."

"Right on the money, Jack," Borodine said.

Boxer looked to his Russian counterpart. "I have the conn," he said without hesitation.

Borodine nodded, yielding command. He moved quietly from the chair and let Boxer slide in.

"Sark . . . get this up on the array."

"Aye, aye, sir," Sarkis replied, his hands flying across computer console buttons.

In a matter of seconds, the large UWIS system had converted the tactical situation to a graphic. The two *Alfas* had the *SW* at right angles to them. Each was at about a nine-mile range. Boxer was sure that the leading *Alfa* . . . the one he had named *Costello* . . . had started a turn and was heading back to a targeting position. He was going to have to think of something fast.

Nine miles to the south, Captain Kalienko was about to order battle stations when he monitored the active ping of *Krieg* Three. He did not like the way that T'Sung had announced his presence. The American would surely be zeroing a torpedo or missile on the Chinese skipper now. Meanwhile, he would wait.

"All stop. Rig for silent running."

"I'll be in my cabin. When the American gets to five miles . . . call me."

Yuri was just entering the CR as Kalienko was getting out of the commander's seat.

"You have the conn, Yuri." He repeated his order about being awakened at five miles.

Yuri yawned and nodded, pulling the Walkman headset from his ears.

He slipped into the seat. "I have the conn," he said. "Give me a weapons status check." The chief of the boat started to check missile and torpedo conditions. When they had to engage the American they would have no time to cope with snarls in their systems.

Abruptly, Yuri felt a stabbing pain in his left temple. "Tell the pharmacist's mate to get me something for a headache."

Boxer looked at the array with Borodine. "What do you think? They have no equivalent of the Sea Dart, right?"

"Correct," the Russian said. "But, the torpedo is a good homing one. We encountered them before and the only thing that separated us from the bottom was that thermocline."

"I assume that there is no thermocline here. You checked?" Boxer asked.

The Russian shook his head. "It was the first thing I checked. We have lots of water under us, but there is little in the way of a hiding place."

"Attack analysis, Igor?"

"Ours or theirs."

"Theirs, of course," Boxer answered.

"A right angle attack is a textbook situation. When capital ships used it, they called the maneuver

'Crossing the T.' It allowed the big guns to fire through the line of approaching ships."

"So, they coordinate a spread . . . what six to a side?"

The Russian nodded. "As many as they can get into the water."

Boxer looked at the array on the screen. "Just waiting for us to get into range, then?"

"We have a range edge on our torpedoes. But, not a large one," Igor responded.

"I wonder if this new bozo knows that?" Boxer asked, rhetorically. "Perhaps that's what we should call him. *Bozo* on the flank and *Costello* in front of us."

"Very well," Sarkis, said, already coding the name into the computer. Sarkis suddenly blinked.

"Transients on . . . ah . . . *Bozo,* Skipper."

There was dead silence in the CR.

"How many, Sark?" Boxer asked.

"Four . . . now five . . . make it six. Yes, six. A full spread. They seem to be running hot, straight, and normal."

"Silent running," Boxer snapped. "Might as well not ring a cowbell for them."

"Silent running, aye," Billingsly responded.

"What's happening with the fish?" Boxer asked Sarkis.

"Torpedoes are seeking. One has acquired. Two have acquired." He took off the headset and looked to Boxer. "Four have acquired, Captain."

"What about the other two?"

"I have a detonation in the water at the range that

213

it was when I last checked. It hit something . . . a whale of a piece of wreckage. I have lost sonar contact with the sixth. She perhaps sank. Engine malfunctioned. It happens with these. They're sensitive but cranky."

Boxer looked to Borodine for confirmation and the Russian nodded. "Numbers say one in six *will* do that."

"Four hot and two dead. Crank up noisemakers and give me revs for flank speed. Make course zero nine zero. We'll make *Costello* recalibrate before he fires. He has to in a matter of minutes."

The huge *SW* props churned water and the sub dashed ahead at forty knots. *Bozo's* torpedoes would be close to out of fuel by the time that they reached the *SW.*

"Is there any action from *Costello,* Sarkis?" Boxer called.

Sarkis adjusted the UWIS. "Nothing, sir. He went to silent running at about nine miles. He may be trying to sit this one out the way he sat the last one out."

"Hope he does. If he fires a spread, we'll have all kinds of shit on our hands. Time to impact on the spread?"

"Six minutes, thirty seconds, Jack," Borodine had slipped beside Sarkis and was helping with the calibrations.

"Get me a firing solution on *Bozo* . . . both torp and Sea Dart."

It only took Sarkis and the computer a matter of seconds to come up with the answer. As he passed it to his captain, the information was heading into the computers in the torpedo and missile warheads. They would update until the second before firing.

"Solution plotted, Skipper."

"Fire torps and Sea Dart. Reload all tubes immediately."

"Aye, sir," Sarkis said almost absently.

Boxer could feel the *SW* buck slightly as the torpedoes were fired in a blast of compressed air. A second later, the container that housed the Sea Dart was expelled upward from the firing tube that had once housed an ICBM. As it broke through the surface, the Sea Dart accepted its commands from its computer and started a long parabolic run that would drop it back into the sea hopefully, right above *Bozo*.

"Four torpedoes inbound, Captain. Hot straight and normal. ETA is now five minutes," Borodine reported as he read data from the UWIS.

"Put that time on the computer clock. Get a reading every thirty seconds. What's happening with *Costello*, Sarkis?"

The tall executive officer shrugged and shook his head. "Not a thing, Skipper. She's in about the volume of water where we had her placed. But, she's still in the weeds and there seems to be no action in her armament system. We will get a few seconds warning before she fires because I'll be able to hear her open her outer doors."

"Have you probed with active?"

"Not yet, sir."

"Might as well. We're making enough noise to wake up the dead anyway."

Sonar pulses started to pinpoint the exact position of *Costello*.

On *Krieg* Three, Kalienko was on his feet and heading back to the control room as soon as the first sonar pulse slammed into the hull.

"Yuri, get me a firing solution on the American." He looked to the small man who was having a hard time getting up from the captain's seat.

"What's the matter with you? Are you all right?"

Yuri waved the questions away and started to the TDC to do the preliminary calculations. It took him a few minutes, but he managed to get the figures in.

"Plotted," he reported weakly.

Kalienko looked closely at his second in command. What he did not need now was slow response for any reason. He would be forced to surrender the experience of Yuri for the speed of another officer. "You're relieved, Yuri. Get below. Have Constintine lay up to the CR on the double."

The small Russian did not like being away from the action as they were about to go into combat. But, he also knew that the pain he was experiencing was starting to interfere with his vision and he was going to have to go below.

"Very well, sir."

"When you start to feel up to it, get back up here."

"I will, sir." Yuri obediently headed below.

"Three minutes to impact," the metallic voice called over the intercom.

"What about the impact on the *Bozo?*" Boxer asked.

Sarkis turned for the console. "Sea Dart back in the water."

"What about our spread of torpedoes," the American admiral asked.

"Four minutes. We might not see them hit." Sarkis's gallows humor was terrifying. It was something Boxer had not heard in some time. He never knew whether he dreaded it or enjoyed it. "Skipper! *Bozo*'s trying an emergency blow. Sea Dart is closing. She's going to try to pass her. Dart turning . . . matching speed. . . ."

Sarkis paused for a second that seemed like an eternity.

"What, Sarkis? What have you got?" Boxer yelled.

"Two minutes thirty seconds," the computer chirped.

"Impact. Blew her to shit. Implosion . . . breaking up noises."

There was a cheer in the CR that was stopped by the sudden announcement.

"Two minutes to impact!"

Borodine turned from his console. "Jack, *Costello* has flooded her tubes."

"Has she opened outer doors?" Boxer queried.

"No. Not yet," Igor answered. "Only a matter of

seconds, though. They have to have heard the hit on *Bozo.*"

Billingsly was slamming a fist into the console.

"Goddamn it. Skipper, we have a malfunction on the last Sea Dart. We're down to torps."

"One minute thirty seconds."

"Get a firing solution on *Costello,*" Boxer ordered.

"Already plotted," Sarkis answered.

"Fire a full spread when ready," Boxer said.

Sarkis started hitting the firing studs after flipping up their red protective covers.

"Four fish gone . . . running hot straight and normal, sir," Sarkis reported.

"Very well."

"One minute to torpedo impact."

"Noisemakers at thirty seconds, Igor. What's our depth?"

"One hundred fifty feet, sir," the helmsman answered.

"I want an emergency blow at fifteen seconds. Right full rudder and hold flank speed."

The helmsman repeated the words as he spun the wheel and turned the engine room signal knob to the right.

"Sir, I have what I think is *Costello* opening her outer doors," Sarkis said. It was what Boxer had hoped he would not hear. Taking them on *one at a time* was something he and this *SW* could do. Two at a time was potentially deadly.

"Thirty seconds to impact!"

"Does she know we fired?"

"She has to know now, sir," Billingsly answered.

"All of our fish have acquired on her doors opening. They are homing."

"Fifteen seconds to torpedo impact."

"Fire noisemakers and release decoys. Emergency blow!" Boxer bellowed.

The *SW* swung upward as all of her ballast was jettisoned at once. The four torpedoes that were boring in on her position veered slightly to adjust themselves to the changing position of the target. Four decoys were sprayed in all directions and they immediately started to signal relentlessly that each of them was actually the *SW*.

Three of the torpedoes took the bait. Confused by the noisemakers, they bore in on one of the decoys and exploded only feet away. Five hundred feet above where the falling decoy had been hit, the *SW* was screaming for the surface. The last torpedo was swinging back on her trail. She had somehow managed to separate the *SW* signal from the cacophony of sound that was in the water now.

"Left full rudder. Maybe we can get her to pass us and have to turn. She has to be low on fuel."

"Left full rudder, aye."

"What's going on with *Costello,* Igor?"

"Tubes flooded . . . outer doors open. She's going to have to figure out what to do with our fish, though. They are closing on her."

"Torpedo turning onto our new course."

"Distance?"

"Three hundred yards . . . closing at a yard a second," Sarkis answered.

Three seconds later the torpedo exploded.

The blast hit the *SW* in the rear and it was a tribute to her construction that it did not rip her tail off. Emergency bells clanged everywhere as watertight doors closed.

"Damage report," Boxer yelled.

"Integrity is good," Igor reported. "Flooding in the aft torpedo and engineering spaces. Reactor secure. Two dead in after tube room. Three injured. Computers are wiped. Sonar works but targeting and ECM response are all gone."

Boxer nodded silently as he pulled himself from the deck and back into the commander's chair. There was no way they could fire noisemakers. They were defenseless.

"How is *Costello* reacting to the fish?" he asked hopefully.

"Firing decoys," Sarkis reported.

"What else?" Boxer asked. Their survival rested on the reactions of *Costello's* captain.

"Multiple explosions. The fish went for the decoys."

It was Boxer's and the other's death knell. All *Costello's* skipper had to do now was fire the torps he'd loaded minutes before.

"Take her down to ninety feet. All ahead flank . . . if we can make that and steer zero zero zero!"

Boxer's order was designed to turn the *SW* away from what was bound to be a rain of torpedoes from the *Alfa*.

"Engineering reports we can't make flank. We can manage two thirds," the helmsman reported.

"I'll take whatever I can get," Boxer answered.

On *Krieg* Three Kalienko looked at his display.
"Standby to fire."

"Aye, sir," Constintine answered.

Suddenly, alarm bells and Klaxons started to
sound. Red warning lights flashed throughout the
ship. It was a rarely heard warning but a terrifying
one. It was a radiation alert.

"Give me a status report," Kalienko demanded.

A voice from the intercom was the chief engineer's
relaying the disastrous events.

"It was Yuri. He went into the containment area
of the reactor and started pulling control rods. We're
flooded with radiation. Yuri simply walked into the
reactor. Get us to the surface. We have to get out of
here. We're at three hundred rads an hour and rising."

"Emergency surface."

With the diversion of the radiation emergency, the
American sub became suddenly less important. By
the time Kalienko managed to get the boat to the
surface, everything was contaminated. All of the radiation badges, even the ones on the control room
crew were black and off the top of the scale. They
were all going to die.

The *SW* never caught sight of *Costello* again. They
did get high radiation readings in the area and sus-
pected that *Costello* might have a reactor problem.
Beyond that they knew nothing. There were no

more attacks in the Java strike. No one would realize that Yuri had simply jumbled the order of the tapes that he had been listening to since they had gone to sea. He had been triggered early. The only one who had a hint as to what had happened was Eric Von Stempler.

Eric was furious. He had ordered the slow and painful death of Von Kleist. The man's system had failed him and it had cost him a great deal of money.

Just now, though, Eric was starting to suffer from a violent headache.

He stabbed at the intercom. "Tell them to turn off that damn Muzak system," he told his secretary. "And, get me something for a headache."

Fifteen minutes later, Eric Von Stempler leapt from the twenty-seventh floor window of his office. His death, an apparent suicide was never fully explained.

Boxer and Borodine stood on the sail as the *SW* limped her way back into San Francisco and Mare Island.

"You know, Igor, that sub out there had us and never took advantage. Hard to figure. Luck you think?"

"Yes," his Russian colleague agreed. "Certainly not our skill."

"It might have been the last of it, Igor."

"The last of what?"

"The last of the luck that we've been flying on for years."

"I don't know. We might not have too much submariner's luck left. But, you have other kinds."

"What kinds, Igor?" Boxer asked sincerely.

"Carol. You have Carol."

"Yes, I do, don't I? Maybe that's all the luck I'll need for the rest of my life."